The Devil—
With Wings

SELECTED FICTION WORKS BY
L. RON HUBBARD

FANTASY
The Case of the Friendly Corpse

Death's Deputy

Fear

The Ghoul

The Indigestible Triton

Slaves of Sleep & The Masters of Sleep

Typewriter in the Sky

The Ultimate Adventure

SCIENCE FICTION
Battlefield Earth

The Conquest of Space

The End Is Not Yet

Final Blackout

The Kilkenny Cats

The Kingslayer

The Mission Earth Dekalogy*

Ole Doc Methuselah

To the Stars

ADVENTURE
The Hell Job series

WESTERN
Buckskin Brigades

Empty Saddles

Guns of Mark Jardine

Hot Lead Payoff

A full list of L. Ron Hubbard's
novellas and short stories is provided at the back.

*Dekalogy—a group of ten volumes

L. RON HUBBARD

The Devil— *With* Wings

GALAXY PRESS

Published by
Galaxy Press, LLC
7051 Hollywood Boulevard, Suite 200
Hollywood, CA 90028

Printed in the United States of America.

ISBN-10 1-59212-309-0
ISBN-13 978-1-59212-309-4

Library of Congress Control Number: 2007927529

Contents

Stories from Pulp Fiction's Golden Age

A ND it *was* a golden age.

The 1930s and 1940s were a vibrant, seminal time for a gigantic audience of eager readers, probably the largest per capita audience of readers in American history. The magazine racks were chock-full of publications with ragged trims, garish cover art, cheap brown pulp paper, low cover prices—and the most excitement you could hold in your hands.

"Pulp" magazines, named for their rough-cut, pulpwood paper, were a vehicle for more amazing tales than Scheherazade could have told in a million and one nights. Set apart from higher-class "slick" magazines, printed on fancy glossy paper with quality artwork and superior production values, the pulps were for the "rest of us," adventure story after adventure story for people who liked to *read*. Pulp fiction authors were no-holds-barred entertainers—real storytellers. They were more interested in a thrilling plot twist, a horrific villain or a white-knuckle adventure than they were in lavish prose or convoluted metaphors.

The sheer volume of tales released during this wondrous golden age remains unmatched in any other period of literary history—hundreds of thousands of published stories in over nine hundred different magazines. Some titles lasted only an issue or two; many magazines succumbed to paper shortages during World War II, while others endured for decades yet. Pulp fiction remains as a treasure trove of stories you can read, stories you can love, stories you can remember. The stories were driven by plot and character, with grand heroes, terrible villains, beautiful damsels (often in distress), diabolical plots, amazing places, breathless romances. The readers wanted to be taken beyond the mundane, to live adventures far removed from their ordinary lives—and the pulps rarely failed to deliver.

In that regard, pulp fiction stands in the tradition of all memorable literature. For as history has shown, good stories are much more than fancy prose. William Shakespeare, Charles Dickens, Jules Verne, Alexandre Dumas—many of the greatest literary figures wrote their fiction for the readers, not simply literary colleagues and academic admirers. And writers for pulp magazines were no exception. These publications reached an audience that dwarfed the circulations of today's short story magazines. Issues of the pulps were scooped up and read by over thirty million avid readers each month.

Because pulp fiction writers were often paid no more than a cent a word, they had to become prolific or starve. They also had to write aggressively. As Richard Kyle, publisher and editor of *Argosy*, the first and most long-lived of the pulps, so pointedly explained: "The pulp magazine writers, the best of them, worked for markets that did not write for critics or attempt to satisfy timid advertisers. Not having to answer to anyone other than their readers, they wrote about human beings on the edges of the unknown, in those new lands the future would explore. They wrote for what we would become, not for what we had already been."

Some of the more lasting names that graced the pulps include H. P. Lovecraft, Edgar Rice Burroughs, Robert E. Howard, Max Brand, Louis L'Amour, Elmore Leonard, Dashiell Hammett, Raymond Chandler, Erle Stanley Gardner, John D. MacDonald, Ray Bradbury, Isaac Asimov, Robert Heinlein—and, of course, L. Ron Hubbard.

In a word, he was among the most prolific and popular writers of the era. He was also the most enduring—hence this series—and certainly among the most legendary. It all began only months after he first tried his hand at fiction, with L. Ron Hubbard tales appearing in *Thrilling Adventures, Argosy, Five-Novels Monthly, Detective Fiction Weekly, Top-Notch, Texas Ranger, War Birds, Western Stories,* even *Romantic Range.* He could write on any subject, in any genre, from jungle explorers to deep-sea divers, from G-men and gangsters, cowboys and flying aces to mountain climbers, hard-boiled detectives and spies. But he really began to shine when he turned his talent to science fiction and fantasy of which he authored nearly fifty novels or novelettes to forever change the shape of those genres.

Following in the tradition of such famed authors as Herman Melville, Mark Twain, Jack London and Ernest Hemingway, Ron Hubbard actually lived adventures that his own characters would have admired—as an ethnologist among primitive tribes, as prospector and engineer in hostile climes, as a captain of vessels on four oceans. He even wrote a series of articles for *Argosy,* called "Hell Job," in which he lived and told of the most dangerous professions a man could put his hand to.

Finally, and just for good measure, he was also an accomplished photographer, artist, filmmaker, musician and educator. But he was first and foremost a *writer,* and that's the L. Ron Hubbard we come to know through the pages of this volume.

This library of Stories from the Golden Age presents the best of L. Ron Hubbard's fiction from the heyday of storytelling, the Golden Age of the pulp magazines. In these eighty volumes, readers are treated to a full banquet of 153 stories, a kaleidoscope of tales representing every imaginable genre: science fiction, fantasy, western, mystery, thriller, horror, even romance—action of all kinds and in all places.

Because the pulps themselves were printed on such inexpensive paper with high acid content, issues were not meant to endure. As the years go by, the original issues of every pulp from *Argosy* through *Zeppelin Stories* continue crumbling into brittle, brown dust. This library preserves the L. Ron Hubbard tales from that era, presented with a distinctive look that brings back the nostalgic flavor of those times.

L. Ron Hubbard's Stories from the Golden Age has something for every taste, every reader. These tales will return you to a time when fiction was good clean entertainment and the most fun a kid could have on a rainy afternoon or the best thing an adult could enjoy after a long day at work.

Pick up a volume, and remember what reading is supposed to be all about. Remember curling up with a *great story*.

—Kevin J. Anderson

KEVIN J. ANDERSON *is the author of more than ninety critically acclaimed works of speculative fiction, including The Saga of Seven Suns, the continuation of the Dune Chronicles with Brian Herbert, and his* New York Times *bestselling novelization of L. Ron Hubbard's* Ai! Pedrito!

The Devil—
With Wings

The Devil—
With Wings

CAPTAIN ITO SHINOHARI
HERO IN KILLING OF *AKUMA-NO-HANÉ*

TOKYO, JAPAN—May 9 (Tekko News Agency)— General Ytosho Shimokado, commanding Japanese Imperial Troops at Port Arthur, Manchukuo, announced today that *Akuma-no-Hané,* infamous white pilot, was killed last week near the Amur River.

Captain Ito Shinohari, famous and gallant figure of the Imperial Japanese Military Intelligence, was credited with the slaying.

Akuma-no-Hané, "The Devil With Wings," has long conducted his lawless operations against the Manchukuo government and, it is reported, recently attempted to bring about the overthrow of the Son of Heaven, whose gentle rule of Manchukuo is well-known.

It is also rumored that *Akuma-no-Hané* was in the pay of Russia and played considerable part in instigating the recent clash of arms between Japan and Russia in the unknown reaches of the Amur River.

A will-o'-the-wisp figure, the as yet unidentified renegade will long be remembered for his three-year reign of terror.

The details of the slaying have not been reported. It is said that Captain Ito Shinohari will be rewarded with the Order of the Rising Sun.

CHAPTER ONE

The Night Marauder

DARKNESS and silence lay like velvet paws upon the Japanese Intelligence Headquarters at Port Arthur.

The far-off midnight hum of the city did not reach into these musty, tomblike corridors or touch the dungeon files wherein lay the yellowing bones of countless "Asiatic incidents."

The blue chill of moonlight seeped cautiously in through a grimy window to touch a pencil of shining steel, the bayonet of the sentry.

The Japanese dozed against his rifle, mustard-colored cap pulled down to leave only the highlights of his cheekbones visible.

He was dreaming, perhaps, of glory to be won in Manchukuo. Or of the fair ladies of Nippon. More probably he dreamed of nothing, trained as he was until he marched and ate and talked like a life-size military doll.

A tread softer than a cat's sounded below him on the steps. He did not look up. Mice were too frequently out in patrols to forage through the gloom of this dingy building.

A board creaked forlornly and still the sentry did not turn.

A shadow crossed the gleaming pearl of the moon and melted against the dark silence. The sentry shifted his gun and looked up, conscious of a curious prickling sensation along the base of his skull.

A hand in a black glove came over the sentry's shoulder and touched the insignia there. The Japanese stiffened, whirled. His strap slapped and his boots grated as he brought his rifle up.

Moonlight sparkled on the butt of a .45 automatic. The bayonet lanced upward toward a space of white throat.

The sentry grunted and sagged back. The black glove caught the released rifle in midair before it could clatter against the floor and then laid it down beside the relaxed Japanese soldier.

Gary Forsythe wasted no time inspecting his handiwork. He stood up in the patch of moonlight and looked down the steps up which he had come. To a Japanese, Forsythe would have looked like a giant, though he was only half an inch over six feet. He would have given any observing yellow man a shock in other ways besides size.

From Shanghai to Vladivostok, the sight of this black-garbed white man had, for three years, been occasion for various types of heart failure among the soldiers of the Rising Sun.

Gary Forsythe

Of his face only his nostrils and mouth were visible. The black leather flying helmet and the huge goggles were more effective than any mask. The black artillery boots looked staunch and solid but he could walk like a panther in them.

There were only three spots of light about him: the lens of each goggle and the large silver buckle of his belt.

His lips curved downward into a chilly grin as he stepped noiselessly over the Japanese and slid silent as a thundercloud along the black passageway.

He turned a corner and came to a stop. The glazed glass of one door exuded a thin yellow light, diffused until it spread like a saffron fog through the gloom. The ideograph on the door said, "Records."

Forsythe reached toward the knob but an instant before he touched it, a shadow became sharply outlined on the other side. The cap and profile of a Japanese, the silhouette of a fixed bayonet.

Instead of touching the knob, Forsythe stepped closer and made a fist of his glove.

He knocked sharply and the sound of it went booming through the brooding structure like a war drum.

The silhouette straightened and turned. The knob rattled. Yellow light spread from top to bottom in a long, widening line. The sentry stood there with bayonet at ready, peering into the gloom.

He saw the tall black shadow before him, caught the terrifying glitter of the goggles. The sentry needed no time for decision. He lunged and light streaked down the cold steel.

Forsythe stepped nimbly aside. He knew bayonets.

The gloves gripped the barrel as the bayonet dashed past. With a wrench, Forsythe whipped the weapon out of the sentry's hands and delivered a vicious butt stroke to the jaw.

Forsythe placed the rifle against the wall and stepped over the Japanese and into the Records room.

An unshaded electric light was burning above a littered, scarred table. The walls were lined with the tarnished brass handles of the files.

Without hesitation he strode to a cabinet and jerked it open. The black gloves gathered up large handfuls of paper to throw them upward and back. The sheets rustled and settled like enormous snowflakes over the rug.

Forsythe located the file he required and chuckled softly as he read his name blazoned in large ideographs across the top of it: THE DEVIL WITH WINGS.

He stepped to the table and started to sit down. A sound held him crouched for an instant and then he straightened up and paced to the window and studied the street below.

A chunky Japanese car had drawn up to the curb before the office and now three officers were getting out. They looked squat and bearish in their greatcoats under the hard light from the street lamp.

Looking down at their precise round hats, Forsythe tried to recognize them. They stood talking for several seconds and then the leanest one of the lot started toward the entrance of the building. He looked up just before he stepped inside.

Forsythe drew hastily back.

It was Shinohari of the Japanese Intelligence.

The other two officers stayed by the car.

Forsythe paced again to the table and ripped into the file he had found. He tossed papers to the right and left until he came upon a thick wad of posters. He crammed a number of these into his jacket and then raced his glance across a clip of letters, singling out a pair, one of which read:

Captain Ito Shinohari
Imperial Japanese Army Headquarters

Honorable Sir:
    The American engineer Robert Weston was murdered yesterday near Aigun on the Amur River. Evidence indicates that he was killed by The Devil With Wings, *Akuma-no-Hané.*

N-38 at Aigun
Decoded by Lt. Tatsu
April 2

The other said:

Captain Shinohari:
    Enclosed herewith a letter from Robert Weston to one Patricia Weston, his sister, mentioning value of a Confucius image. Original letter forwarded to Patricia Weston. As image may contain some secret document, suggest you follow lead to Patricia Weston. The hand of *Akuma-no-Hané* is quite plain in this.

Colonel Shimizu
Commanding Aigun
April 6

He wadded these into a small packet and slipped them into the heavy money belt at his waist.

For a moment he stood listening, looking at the door. He knew that Shinohari would find the unconscious sentry at the top of the steps, but *Akuma-no-Hané* preferred to let events take their own course.

Again he shuffled through the papers, watching for any detail which might serve him well. He missed the copy of the original letter to Patricia Weston though he tried hard to find it.

Another communication came under his hand:

Captain Ito Shinohari
Imperial Japanese Army Intelligence
Port Arthur

Honorable Sir:

May this unworthy agent be allowed to report that, after two days of constant watching, Patricia Weston has not yet contacted *Akuma-no-Hané*. May this one humbly request relief from his post, knowing he can better serve the gallant Captain in other departments better.

In information it has been learned that Patricia Weston is without funds and it is not likely that she will leave Port Arthur. As ordered, this one has carefully undermined her credit at her hotel and at the cable station. There is therefore no likelihood of her leaving, or communicating with any possible friends in the United States.

This one suggests that it might be prudent to cause her to be deported at government expense.

N-16 at Port Arthur
May 3

Akuma-no-Hané slid this with the others into his money belt. He slapped the file into chaos about the room and strode to the Records office door, .45 drawn.

Before he could reach the knob it slammed toward him!

Shinohari, Luger in hand, was framed in the opening. Three feet from him Forsythe had centered the muzzle of the .45 automatic upon the yellow greatcoat.

They stood there, deadlocked, glaring at each other.

It was Shinohari who first recognized the stalemate. His small pockmarked face wreathed into a smile which was no deeper than his teeth. His metallic, obsidian eyes remained very calm.

"The Devil," said Shinohari, "With Wings."

Forsythe bowed mockingly from the waist. "The gallant Captain Shinohari."

"Of course. I am so sorry I did not know you were coming. I might have arranged a suitable reception for you, worthy of your fame."

"I grieve that I did not apprise you of the fact, Captain. May I extend my apologies for being delinquent in paying my respects recently, Captain?"

Captain Shinohari

Shinohari bowed and clicked his heels. "It has been so long since I have had the pleasure of meeting you, sir."

"My regrets for your sometimes, shall we say, hasty marksmanship, Captain."

"If I could but match your excellent accuracy, sir, I should be a most happy man." The black eyes never left Forsythe's face, the Luger did not waver an inch. "You have doubtless been amusing yourself against my coming?"

"Quite," replied Forsythe. "You have a great deal of correspondence. You must be as busy as you are great, Captain."

"Thank you. I am rarely bored, sir. Your health? It is excellent?"

"Quite, Captain. I regret—"

"Oh, no, no, no. Regret nothing, sir. I am desolated that I was not here to receive you more properly. I . . . er . . . have been taking considerable interest in your recent itinerary, sir."

"You flatter my poor efforts, Captain."

"I am prostrated not to be able to attend your various calls in person. The Imperial Japanese government is quite attentive to your goings and comings, sir. You are . . . shall we say . . . a very great man. A power, as it were, in Northern Asia."

"You flatter me," replied Forsythe with a slight bow. "If my fame were only a tenth of your own, I should be content."

"These guns," said Shinohari, "are rather foolish, don't you think? When the great meets the great, they should not demean themselves with common brawling."

"I suggest," said Forsythe politely, "that we unload together.

12

I regret that I did not have time to put a shell under my firing pin."

"Strange coincidence," said Shinohari. "I was too startled to think of it and my Luger is in a like condition."

They bowed together and then each one placed his left hand before him with great ostentation and slowly curved it in under his automatic.

"Shall we say at the count of three?" said Forsythe.

"Splendid. Shall we count together?"

"One . . . two . . . three . . ."

Twin clicks were sharp in the room. Two magazines slid out of the butts and into the reaching hands. Timing their movements exactly, they each placed the clips in their belts and lowered their automatics.

"I regret," said Forsythe with a smile as brittle as the captain's, "that I cannot stay. I have an urgent appointment elsewhere."

"I also must extend my regrets," said Shinohari with a bow. "I only came for the files of a new incident."

"May I wish you success?" said Forsythe, moving toward the door.

"Thank you. And may great success attend your endeavors, dear sir."

At the sill they bowed again, black jacket toward yellow greatcoat. They smiled as they went around until Forsythe had his back to the hall and the captain's to the room.

Still bowing and still backing, Forsythe went toward the corner and halfway around it.

Abruptly the captain raised his Luger. He had carefully forgotten the shell under his firing pin until now.

Forsythe saw the motion and dodged around the corner. The bullet slapped the plaster close beside his face.

He leveled his .45 and squeezed. The captain was hastily throwing himself backward and out of sight. Forsythe's bullet sent the glass from the door in a stinging, glittering shower.

Forsythe had also forgotten his loaded chamber.

He whirled and raced down toward the steps. The officers by the car would be on the alert and he had to pass them. Behind him he heard a window crash open. The captain's shrill voice blasted a warning down at the sidewalk.

Forsythe took the steps four at a time, almost soaring through the blackness on the wings of his wind-harried jacket. He sped into the lower corridor and stopped just inside the main door, hastily loading his .45.

The two officers were stepping stiffly toward the entrance, watchful, guns in hand.

Forsythe leaped into sight.

One officer fired too fast, the other was too slow.

The .45 roared twice, the explosions blurring together. One Japanese sprawled out at full length. The other sagged slowly to his knees, still trying to bring up his gun.

The chauffeur leaped out of the car, stung to action by the yapping staccato of orders from the captain above. The chauffeur drew and chopped a frightened shot at the black terror which was streaking toward him off the steps.

Forsythe fired into the chauffeur's face and whipped around to stab two more bullets at the window.

14

The captain dodged back, shooting as he went at the small moving target under him.

Forsythe leaped into cover behind the car. He was waiting for the captain above to show himself again, but that intelligent intelligence officer was not given to foolhardy chances except when absolutely necessary. He made no appearance.

With a slow, amused grin, Forsythe drew out a poster and carefully slid it under the windshield wiper of the car.

He sent one more shot at the empty window and then rocketed down the street and out of sight into an alley. The sound of his boots faded out.

The chilly, hard light from the arc lamp beat down on three sprawled bodies and upon the white poster which read:

$50,000 GOLD

WILL BE PAID BY

THE IMPERIAL JAPANESE GOVERNMENT
FOR THE HEAD OF THE DEVIL WITH WINGS

Wanted for:
Shooting down KDA-5 Pursuit plane at Harbin.
Derailing Imperial troop-train at Mukden.
Murder of Chinese advisor Shu-Sen.
Bombing Jelhi.
Killing government agent N-38 URGA.
High treason.
Espionage.
The murder of Robert Weston in Mongolia.
The killing of four . . .

Captain Shinohari stepped over the bodies on the walk and stood for some time looking at the poster.

He drew his lips back from his teeth and looked off into the northwest. A sign swinging in the wind against the cold moon made a silhouette like a gibbet.

CHAPTER TWO

Vengeance

THE room was aloof from the rest of the café. The light which came from the table lamp did not reach higher than a man's thighs, leaving the odd impression that the room was only half-real, cutting the tables and chairs off at the halfway mark and showing up nothing above that point.

Forsythe's belt buckle was the only thing which marked his presence at a smaller table against the wall—the buckle and the toes of his outwardly sprawled black boots. Above that, Forsythe was a part of the dimness.

Through the partly opened door he could see the main room of the café. It was a smoky, blurred sight, knifed here and there by the colored gowns of the singsong girls who moved and made green and yellow and red patches against the somber gowns of the Chinese men.

A fife and a fiddle with a snakeskin head could be heard shrilly accompanying the high-pitched voices of unseen singers, who ranged up and down the Chinese music scale to tell a story of two warriors lost in a far country and dreaming of home.

The underlying buzz of conversation was as jerky as the music.

But that was in the main room. The sill of the door marked

a boundary between the carefree drinkers and the silently waiting Forsythe.

A waiter cautiously slid into the cubicle and placed hot rice wine timorously beside the hand of the mute Forsythe.

Forsythe's hand moved into the light. It was a slender hand, suggesting in its quick strength a Toledo blade. He raised the glass up into the darkness and set it back again—empty.

The waiter sidled out. For an instant the door was thrown wide and the outside beams spread across Forsythe's features. He had removed his helmet and goggles and without their gruesomeness, he looked young, not more than thirty. His hair was sun-bleached and unruly. The eyes were deeply set into the striking face—eyes as pale as the silver of his buckle. Eyes which betokened crystal intelligence and capabilities. . . .

Few men were brave enough to talk about those capabilities.

The door shut and then burst open with a suddenness which sent Forsythe's hand stabbing toward his holster. The fingers relaxed and came back to the table.

"Forsythe!" said the newcomer excitedly.

"Shut the door, Ching."

"Sure. You bet. I'm sorry. Looky here, Forsythe. . . ."

"Sit down and cool off."

Ching was too excited to do that. He leaned across the table and stared through the lamplight with black eyes which snapped with eagerness. He was young, was Ching. He was an idealist. He had lost his Oriental calm at Yale.

"Forsythe, there's a woman looking for you."

"What sort of a woman?"

"And the Japanese are spreading the net for you. We've got to get out of Port Arthur."

"That's what they expect us to do."

"Sure," said Ching. "But, gee whiz, you can't stick around here and get yourself bumped off. I just passed a squad in the street. There isn't a place in town they'll leave untouched. What happened?"

"Never mind," said Forsythe. "You mentioned a woman."

"Sure. You bet. An American. She's been going all over Port Arthur asking everybody where she can find *Akuma-no-Hané.*"

"You've seen her?"

"No. Of course not. But a clerk from the steamship office told me that a coolie who knows a waiter in the All Worlds Café who—"

"The grapevine. Certainly. What have you found out about her?"

"Her room-boy told me she's behind with her bill and hasn't eaten for two days. She's high-strung, out of her head because her brother—"

"Why does she want to meet me?"

"Nobody knows. But with the patrols out, I don't think—"

"An American, stranded. . . . What's her name, Ching?"

"Patricia Weston."

Ching thought he saw Forsythe give a start. "Gosh, you know her?"

Forsythe tossed the looted letters before Ching. Ching's eager black eyes soaked up the words, his mouth sagged. "They're nuts! You didn't kill any guy named Weston!" Ching

19

scowled. "They're trying to hang one of their own blunders on you."

"Shinohari never blunders," remarked Forsythe casually. "He controls the Records office. He had a very definite reason for doing away with an American engineer, another reason for making me the goat."

"Political?"

Forsythe was grinning balefully. "Shinohari's reasons in this must have been personal. Japan would not be interested in one lone American engineer, could not risk international complications attendant to his death. Ching, Shinohari is up to something and he's trying to keep it from his superiors. By pinning this killing on me with these false records—"

"Aw," said Ching, "the more I hear from these Japs, the less respect I've got for their noodles. We're trying to oust the well-known son of the universe, Henry Pu Yi. And that hasn't got a thing to do with—"

"You grow careless," said Forsythe. "Ching, I think you had better slip over to her hotel and say that I'm waiting here to see her."

"Maybe she's lined up with the Japanese Intelligence. This may be just another clumsy trap to—"

"She would not be so blatant about contacting me if she was Japanese Intelligence. Bring her here."

Ching shrugged. "Okay. You're the boss. But this is liable to bring our old pal Shinohari right down on our ears."

He went out and closed the door behind him.

Forsythe sat for some time looking into his empty glass and

thinking about nothing in particular. He was not a nervous type and the life he had been leading for the last three years had only schooled him into better self-discipline.

He got up lazily and walked to the washbasin and mirror across the room. He lit the lamp there and held it up at the level of his shoulder, looking at his reflection. The curiosity in his study faded to weariness. He set the light down and poured out some water.

Puzzled with himself, he shaved carefully and then changed his shirt. He raised the lamp once more and looked at himself. He was not very pleased. The black silk was wrinkled and the white ideographs over the pocket were suddenly distasteful to him.

His lean face tightened into a grimace of disgust. He said slowly and mockingly, "The Devil With Wings."

When the door opened again, Forsythe was seated at the small table, his face little more than a white blur by the light which seeped in from the main room.

Silhouetted against the lamp and smoke and shrill music stood Patricia Weston. Not even the bulk of her marten coat could hide the tension of her shapely body.

She seemed to be making a decision and then, with determination, she stepped forward, holding a leather purse in both hands.

Ching followed her and closed the door. He drew out a chair at the main table and seated her in such a way that the light was in her face—making it necessary for her to stare through it to see Forsythe in the darkness beyond.

A chair had scraped and she knew the man had risen. Leather creaked and she saw the silver of his buckle. He was seated again.

Forsythe looked steadily at her, saying nothing. At first he thought he was trying to read the thoughts which might lie behind her eyes, but suddenly he gave up that pretense.

She was beautiful!

He had never before seen eyes like that. They were vivid and deep, the eyes of a woman capable of great love and fury. Looking at her, he realized with a shock that she was not very big. He had thought otherwise. She certainly made the most of her five feet three. Dark strands of her brown hair curled out from under her flippant hat to lie smokily against the paleness of her brow.

He could feel the intensity of her. She was like a swift storm or a blazing sunrise. Her mouth was full and sweet—and impetuous.

With a shock Forsythe realized that his hands were trembling unaccountably.

"You came to see me," said Forsythe with disbelief. "Why?"

"I came to see a man and I find myself staring into darkness."

Her voice was barely controlled and in it there was an undercurrent of anger and decision.

"Of course," said Forsythe. "That's for precaution, you know."

He leaned forward and slid one of the posters under the light. She glanced at it.

"Fifty thousand dollars," she said bitterly. "Why do they add to your ego?"

"You are upset about something," said Forsythe. "Perhaps something I have done?"

She was under a terrific strain as she looked up from the poster.

"'The murder of Robert Weston in Mongolia.'"

"Oh, now, see here," protested Forsythe. "You can't go around believing every impossible rumor you hear. When that happened I was—"

"No! You can't tell me where you were because you were there. You murderer! He was worth a thousand of you! Because you could not otherwise obtain the Confucius—"

"I keep hearing this thing about Confucius. What is it?"

"A smooth liar, too? In keeping with your horrible reputation." Her hands still clutched the bag in her lap.

Ching came around the table to stand beside Forsythe. He was nervous. He had not suspected the vitality of this woman and he was overawed by the way she dared speak to a man who had become legend.

"You are upset," said Forsythe. "I give you my word I had nothing to do with the killing of Weston. Is he your brother?"

"So you even know that!"

"I make it my business to know things. For instance, it would not be wise to take that .25 automatic out of your purse."

Forsythe underestimated her. He had thought to frighten her into forsaking the mission which was now altogether too clear.

She suddenly brought the bag into view, her right hand deep within it.

In a low, throbbing voice, she said, "Don't move."

Ching stiffened. His hand started toward his holster but Forsythe stopped the motion.

Patricia Weston gradually pulled the purse away from in front of the wicked little automatic.

"Robert was all I had," she said. "It was to pay our way out of this country. And then you killed him and left him to the wild dogs. You left me stranded here without money or friends because your rapacious greed—"

"Wait," said Forsythe. "You don't understand. . . ."

"Oh, I understand well enough," she said, getting up slowly, centering the .25 until Forsythe could look straight down the muzzle of it. "But I've gotten past caring what happens to *me*."

"Miss Weston," began Forsythe. "If you thought the blood money—"

"Blood money! I care nothing about that. I would not dirty my purse with it!"

He saw she was going to fire, but he was more amazed at her courage and passion than he was afraid of the bullet.

Her face was a drawn mask.

Ching shouted, "Look out!"

Red sparks ribboned past the lamp. The explosion made the flame leap convulsively and the thunder of the small weapon in those close confines hurt the head.

Three times ragged flame thundered from the small gun and then, as though suddenly realizing the thing she had done, she dropped the .25 and whirled, almost falling to the door.

Light showed in the opening for an instant and vanished.

The small patter of her footsteps melted into the far-off shrilling of the singers and the clink of glasses in the café.

Ching, coming out of his daze, rushed angrily toward the door to follow. He tripped over Forsythe's boots and went sprawling across the pool of light on the floor. He lay there, swearing weakly in a mixture of English and Chinese.

CHAPTER THREE

The Strange Visitor

PATRICIA WESTON lay upon her bed in the Imperial Hotel, her face buried in the graceful curve of her white arm, her dark brown hair shimmering dully in the moonlight which streamed in through the window.

Her shoulders shook from time to time as she fought to regain control of her nerves. She had felt very sick for an hour and then, gradually, her young strength had fought off the weakness.

She had killed a man.

She had not even seen his face, but she had heard his voice. And if her rage and her desire for vengeance had not been so great she might have stopped herself in time.

Now she was worse off than before. Her bill was unpaid and the manager was becoming distantly polite. She had not eaten since the day before yesterday. Maybe the dizzy faintness of hunger had driven her to do the thing she had brooded upon for so long.

She was deeply ashamed of her temper, amazed at the depths she had suddenly found in herself, still unwilling to believe that she had done what she had done.

Yesterday she had started to pawn the pistol. If she only had! But she had been afraid of the police and she had wanted . . .

She pushed her face deeper into the bed, shaken again by

the retrospect of the searing fire she had loosed into a human being.

The moonlight fell in a trapezoid upon the thick rug, broken only by the corner of the bed it touched. And then the moonlight was barred by a blurred shadow which swung slowly over the sill.

Patricia lifted her head, still striving to throw off the memory which shook her. She braced her chin on her hand, staring at the rug, brown hair framing her face.

Abruptly she realized that something lay there which did not belong. Her gaze widened. She was staring at a shadow which lay upside down. The shadow of a round-headed thing which stood upright beside the window.

She threw herself hastily back with a small squeal of terror and stared upward at the man who stood there.

He looked like a demon out of another dimension. All black from boots to cap. Two enormous eyes fully three inches across. Great shining eyes, staring steadily at her.

She scrambled back further.

Forsythe did not move. His gauntleted hands were knuckled to his hips. A strange smile was on his mouth.

She was as far away from him as she could get. Their stares locked. Only the moonlight, reflected up from the floor, showed her to him.

She was dressed in bright blue pajamas, collar and belt in silver, and Forsythe, though he could not see them, knew that her eyes were also blue and dark and growing stormy.

Her voice was vibrant with swiftly rising indignation. "Who are you? What are you doing here?"

Forsythe took another step toward the edge of the bed. "If I were a fortuneteller, Miss Weston, I would say that you were going on a long, long journey."

She recognized his voice with a start which sent cold shivers racing over her. She tried to slide sideways toward the door. She tried to cry out for help.

"Do not shout," said Forsythe. "You are too kindhearted to want to see your room-boy die as he comes through the door."

"They call you . . ."

Somehow Forsythe hated to hear her say it.

She clutched at her creamy throat, terror freezing her. "The Devil—With Wings. I . . . I believe it."

"Don't upset yourself," said Forsythe, trying to be gallant. "I could not call and leave my card, you know. Fifty thousand would be a fortune to a hotel manager—especially when all he had to do was phone Captain Shinohari. Come. We are wasting precious time. Dawn is not three hours away."

"But . . . but I killed you! At that distance I could not miss!"

"You didn't," Forsythe assured her. "Come now, be a good lass and climb into some clothes. You will have a long journey—"

"If you think I'm going anywhere with you, you're crazy!"

Forsythe shrugged. "You're crazy to stay here. No money, you owe the hotel, you haven't eaten. . . . Oh, no, you haven't. I've been hungry too often myself not to recognize the sign of it. Tonight you were hysterical. Only hunger and grief could drive a woman to those lengths. Or perhaps love. Quickly now. You can't take very much. You'll overload the ship as it is."

She did not move, but crouched at the head of the bed watching him move easily toward her bureau and lean against it to light a cigarette.

When the match flared she saw that the "eyes" were huge goggles, and when she saw him blowing out smoke in a very human way, she suddenly relaxed. She had felt so bad about killing him that now she was glad to behold him still alive.

"If you don't mind," said Forsythe, "hurry it up a little. It will be light soon enough and I have no liking for antiaircraft fire—especially with you in the plane."

"I'm not going anywhere—and besides, how can I get dressed with you standing there?"

Forsythe smiled and paced back to the window. As he sat down on the sill and looked out across the rooftops, she saw moonlight strike three metal bulbs which dangled from his wide black belt. They shone brightly as they swung and she knew they were hand grenades. She noted the low-slung holster and saw the protruding dark rectangle of the .45 butt, to which a black lanyard had been hung.

She examined his back curiously, standing slowly up and staring, her small face intent, her head cocked a little on one side.

"Ching has food," remarked Forsythe without turning. "Hot coffee and hot ham sandwiches. It will be cold if you don't hurry."

In spite of herself she licked her lips hungrily. She wondered if she could trust him to stay turned away, and then, seeing the way his shoulders were hunched forward and sensing more than seeing the ripple of animal strength under the black jacket, she snatched up a tweed Shetland wool suit and kicked her shoes ahead of her into the closet.

She left the door open an inch so that she could watch him. He did not turn. He seemed very calm.

Abruptly she was annoyed with him. He had no feelings whatever. Why . . . why, not even a bullet could dent him!

She stepped back into the room and shrugged into her marten coat. She stepped to the mirror and powdered her nose by moonlight. It had not occurred to her to throw the electric switch.

"Remember," said Forsythe, "you go of your own free will."

"I do nothing of the kind," she snapped hotly. "If I resisted, a murderer of your practice would probably strangle me so that you could get away. And . . . and I see no use in getting some poor Chinese killed. You have not heard the last of killing Robert Weston."

"I suppose not," sighed Forsythe, getting up. "All ready?"

"No. Wait. I can't go. It would be dishonest. I owe . . ." She stopped and felt cheap. He was slowly reaching inside his jacket and inside his shirt. She heard snaps pop and then crack as they were put back.

Dull yellow discs glowed in his hand.

He dropped them carelessly in a small shower on the bed.

Her eyes were wide, "Sovereigns!"

"What did you think they were? Cough drops?"

He leaned out of the window and looked carefully down into the street below. The regular tramp-tramp-tramp of a Japanese patrol came around the corner and passed out of sight in another street.

She was still staring at the money. Three coins in the lot had deep dents in their soft metal. He had taken them from a belt about his waist and she had fired at the bright silver buckle of his belt.

"Come on," ordered Forsythe for the tenth time.

She was angry with him again. He took his luck so casually!

She moved nearer to him and he suddenly reached out and stood her up against the window. He whipped a line from nowhere and lashed a harness around her.

He leaned out and whistled shrilly and then guided her on her way.

A moment later she was standing on the roof beside Ching, breathless from dangling over dizzy space. Ching looked appraisingly at her.

"Yes, sir," said Ching with decision. "A lot of broads hung around Yale, but you got them beat from the start."

"You'd better lower that line to your Devil With Wings."

"Sure," said Ching, abashed under the cold scrutiny she gave him.

As he helped Forsythe up over the edge, Ching knew definitely that he hadn't *ever* seen a girl like her. She had nerve enough . . .

"You promised sandwiches?" said Patricia.

"That's better," replied Forsythe, giving Ching a signal.

"What's better about it?" she cried with fury. "Just because I'm hungry enough to eat with pigs is no sign I *am* one!"

Forsythe smiled at her fondly but his goggles made the grin gruesome. She backed away from him, biting at a slice of ham.

Forsythe hurried them down the fire escape, cautioning them to silence. She was not interested in silence or anything in the world that moment but the feeling of food between her small white teeth.

They dropped one by one to the street and Forsythe helped her into a car on which the Rising Sun was emblazoned.

"But this is a staff car!" she said with sudden alarm.

"Of course," said Forsythe.

"It's Shinohari's car," said Ching with pride. "I stole it myself."

"Get going," said Forsythe.

CHAPTER FOUR

Betrayal

T HE staff car pulled to a stop on the edge of a flat field outside Port Arthur. The expanse, dun and common by day, had the appearance of an enormous silver lake under the rays of the waning moon.

The buildings stood in a shadowy, self-effacing huddle, only one white line of light showing between the shutter bottom and a windowsill.

A door opened and spilled an orange flood across the yard. It banged shut and hurried footsteps grew louder. The scarlet of the Rising Sun on the door was not bright in the hazy shimmer of moonbeams. But it was plain.

Panting and frightened, a Chinese with furtive eyes and a thin, cunning face came to an abrupt stop beside the running board. He had come so swiftly from the lighted room and he was so sure of the Rising Sun on the door that he did not give the dark interior before him more than a glance.

"Captain! He is coming here tonight—"

The Chinese stopped his rush of words and took a swift backward step. He was paralyzed by what he had done. Too late he saw the shining crystal ovals which he knew to be the goggles of The Devil With Wings.

Leisurely, Forsythe stepped out of the rear door. Carefully

he closed it behind him. Ching stepped to the ground and casually shut off the lights.

"And so," said Forsythe coolly, "Wong Teh-shui has a different color to the lining of his coat."

The singsong language did not mean anything to Patricia but she felt herself shivering and she could not look away. A cup of coffee and a Thermos bottle in her hands tipped slowly, unattended.

Wong Teh-shui's shifty eyes sought a way out as he gathered the shreds of his courage.

"I was playing Shinohari for you," said Wong nervously. "I have been giving him false leads—"

"False? Anything from you would be false."

"Divine One!" cried Wong, trembling. "This unworthy associate has done nothing which should be punished!"

"Ching," said Forsythe sharply.

Ching stepped slowly to Wong's side and with sudden fury ripped open the man's purple shirt. Wong tried to fall back but Ching held him while he probed into the pockets.

One by one Ching drew out rolls of bills. He dropped them contemptuously into the dust where the wind stirred them and mixed them up into a splotch of green and brown.

"Yen!" said Ching, spitting into the paper at his feet.

"This may account for some of the leaks we have noticed of late," said Forsythe wearily. "You sold the Imperial Advisor Shu-sen out to us. I could expect nothing less in turn. The Japanese have been warned already?"

"NO! NO! I swear they have not!"

"You would swear to anything. For money. Is the plane ready?"

"Please! There is no gas. I did not—"

"Silence," said Forsythe.

"They do not know! I have given them no inkling of why you are trying to unseat Pu Yi—"

"So you sold that, too," said Forsythe. He turned slowly and looked into the car at Patricia.

"I am sorry, Miss Weston. This fellow was an agent and evidently the Japanese know we are to be here tonight. Because of slight haste . . ."

He shrugged and turned away.

Wong's voice was climbing up the scale with terrified breaks. His knees were getting weak and he began to sag against Ching.

"Please, Divine One! Spare me this! Please . . . I did not . . ."

Patricia felt herself grow very cold. The coffee spilled unnoticed from her cup as she unknowingly let it slide from her nerveless hand.

Forsythe had drawn his .45. He carefully took off the safety catch. The metallic click of it was loud all out of proportion to Patricia.

She sensed some titanic struggle here. She knew that Wong was a pawn on the board—a worthless traitor. But even so, the swiftness of the trial, the smallness of the evidence . . .

Everything was hazy in the moonlight as though she saw it through a thick, gauzy curtain of unreality. The tall man in black, the shuddering Chinese now on his knees begging, the impassive Ching.

The trio swam in Patricia's sight. She heard the .45 explode. The shot had been muffled as though something was up against the muzzle. There was no light from it.

A sickish, sweet odor rose up to mingle with the acrid fumes of powder.

Forsythe calmly replaced the empty in his clip. He turned with a weary face to Patricia and opened the door to help her out.

She cowered back from him, shivering, eyes abruptly blazing with untamable fury.

"Please," said Forsythe. "We have but little time. I should not like to have you witness the execution of Ching and myself."

"It would be a pleasure!" she cried wildly.

His hand stabbed inside and caught her wrist. His strong grip would leave fingermarks like a brand on her white flesh. But she gave no sign of pain. She let him drag her out of the car and suffered him to hurry her toward a low building.

Ching slid back what had appeared to be a wall. A big two-seater fighting ship came to view. It was like a hovering vulture in the shadowy hangar. Moonlight gleamed on the metal cowl and upon the twin snouts of machine guns there.

Patricia saw other machine guns on a ring around the rear cockpit. She suddenly stepped back, rebelling.

"Open the hood," said Forsythe.

Ching mounted the stirrup and threw back the bullet-proof glass gunner's hood. The cockpit was large, as a gunner needs room to fire.

She struggled furiously but he only gripped her more tightly.

"I won't go!" she screamed. "You can't do this! I won't!"

His hand was close beside her face. Savagely she sank her teeth into his hard brown wrist. He snatched it away and loosed her and stood back.

She faced him defiantly, feeling she had won.

For seconds they glared at each other, wills bared and clashing.

She stood to the full advantage of her height, chin uptilted, hands thrust defiantly into her pockets. She was daring him to touch her again. Every line of her graceful body showed the taut resentment which flamed within her. Her blue eyes were like twin jets of acetylene and her mouth was a scarlet patch of fury.

Gradually some of the chill of the moonlight began to seep in upon her, shredding the haze of anger which had dropped before her glance to obscure the reality of the world about her.

Slowly she began to see Forsythe in hard, black relief against the eerie light of the silvered field. She felt the effect of the lenses of the goggles. They were twin ovals, blankly facing her, impersonally studying her. Some of the panther strength of the tall outlaw before her began to spread like a sheet of ice into her being.

She dropped her chin ever so slightly. The hands in her pockets were suddenly restive. Her shoulders slowly inched downward as the fire went out.

She was terrified and overawed, facing an unknown, unbending will which had received all her wrath without giving the least sign. There was something ghastly in the inexorable way he stood there, regarding her, seeing straight through her with those impersonal lenses.

Suddenly she felt as though she was unclothed to the cold blast of the Manchurian night. She was alone and weak and helpless, in the grip of a maelstrom of such force that her small strength could avail nothing in its battle against it.

Dejectedly she turned and slowly placed her slippered toe in the stirrup under the rear cockpit.

Ching helped her up and eased her into the wide seat.

Forsythe's tones were casual. "Check the gas, Ching. The fellow was lying, of course."

Ching stepped up on the catwalk and stabbed a flashlight at the fuel gauges. "He wasn't lying! They're *empty*!"

Forsythe stepped a pace ahead and raked the light-splotched interior with anxious eyes. He paced deeply into the hangar, pausing to pick up and shake cans.

Ching cried, "We'd better abandon the plane! Shinohari will be here any minute!"

Forsythe probed deeper into the shadowy corners. He knew that no Chinese would have the courage to waste hundreds of gallons of gasoline.

He felt soft earth under his black boot and instantly knelt to scrape at the floor. Something glittered beneath the covering and he pulled it out to triumphantly hold aloft a full gas tin.

Hurriedly he dug the others out and Ching began to race with them toward the ship.

They gashed the heads with a heavy wrench and spilled the acrid, gurgling fluid into the greedy maw of the tank.

From afar came the throb of an engine, more felt than heard. Ching shot a startled glance at Forsythe and they worked faster.

Forsythe hurled the last tin clattering to the floor and gave Ching a thrust toward the gunner's pit. Black and crouched as a jungle cat, Forsythe stood listening and watching.

The car was coming closer.

Forsythe flung himself into the forward cockpit and threw the switches. The inertia starter began to wheeze and bark and with a chattering, protesting blast, the engine caught and raced into a jangling fanfare of strident sound.

Across the moonlit field a shadow hurtled into sight and skidded to a stop. Other, smaller shadows detached themselves hurriedly and raced toward the hangar.

"Get him!" shrieked a shrill Japanese voice.

Forsythe looked worriedly at his gauges and saw the engine was still too cold. He stood up and unbuckled a grenade from its belt.

Nothing could be heard above the roar of the clanking engine. The shadows swiftly deployed across the open. Lances of orange fire streaked the darkness. Death shrieked close beside Forsythe's head and, cheated, went whining away.

With the slow overhand motion of a softball player, Forsythe looped the grenade into the hazy silver of the field, straight at a close huddle of hurrying soldiery.

The scarlet flash was like a physical blow. Men were silhouetted for an instant against the violence of it and then there was nothing but hovering dust and moonlight.

The firing doubled outside.

Forsythe hooked another grenade far out into the field. It spewed its flame and blast over a wide area. It had been thrown too far and it did no damage.

Forsythe threw himself down into the seat. He unlocked the brakes and struck the throttle with the heel of his hand. A thousand horses beat the air into hurricane ferocity.

The ship lunged through the entrance and charged with red flaring exhausts down the runway.

Shots racketed up from the ground. Holes were magically black in the metal wings.

Ching was standing in the bucking pit, leaning into the kicking recoil of his Matsubi .50-caliber machine gun. Pompoms of blazing vermillion battered the earth.

The huge, glittering empties from the weapon streamed in a hot smoking line not five inches from Patricia's frightened white face.

The attack plane hurtled skyward, nose jabbing toward the cold moon low on the horizon as though the still-spinning wheels could find traction upon the wide path of the silver beams.

Then, at an angle which would have meant suicide to any other pilot than Forsythe, the attack streaked upward at the zenith. The dwindling earth fell swiftly back. The flame of shots below was like flashing bulbs on a switchboard of steel.

As casually as though he stood up naturally instead of standing something less than horizontal, Ching raked the departing world with one last savage burst and then, contemptuously, he clicked the Matsubi's butt into its retaining brackets, sat down, buckled his belt and pulled the hood over the rear pit.

The ship whipped over the hump and level, two thousand feet high, scudding westward to race the first pale streamers of the glowing dawn.

The attack plane hurtled skyward, nose jabbing toward the cold moon low on the horizon as though the still-spinning wheels could find traction upon the wide path of the silver beams.

Ching picked up the inter-cockpit phone. "Are we hit anyplace?"

Forsythe's cold tones came back through the receiver. "Not that I can see. The wings. Did you pot the captain?"

"I doubt it."

"Then there's word on the way to squadrons ahead of us. We fight again before we rest. Keep your guns unlimbered!"

"You bet," grinned Ching. "We'll burn us a couple Nakajimas for breakfast."

"Don't get cocky. Our luck can't last forever."

Ching's smile widened, showing up three gold teeth in his lean face. "Aw, there ain't a Japanese alive that could whip you."

"Trying to dare the little jinxes?"

"Naw, but . . ."

"Entertain the lady and let me fly."

"Okay. I'll keep my peepers peeled for the squadrons."

CHAPTER FIVE

Attacked!

THE fresh coolness of morning spread clear wine across the awakening world. The bleakness of the rolling dun hills was enlivened by the long purple shadows which lay all out of proportion to their mass. In the extreme slant of the sun, ten-foot blocklike houses made dark patches a hundred feet long.

It was an odd world, yellow and immense and grotesque, which held the attention of Patricia Weston. For minutes at a time she stared down upon the weirdness of the shadows and the hazy infinity of horizons.

The hood of shatterproof glass dulled the engine's roar to a lulling murmur. There was no sensation of speed though they traveled at better than two hundred and fifty miles an hour.

She turned and looked questioningly at lean, slangy Ching.

"Where are we going?" she asked.

"Ask *Akuma-no-Hané*. He's taking us there."

"*Akuma-no-Hané?*"

"The Devil With Wings. Don't you talk Japanese?"

"Of course not."

"That's a hell of a note. How'd you get along in Port Arthur?"

"You've been in the United States, haven't you," she decided.

"Sure. Can't you tell Yale's alma mammy when you see one?"

"Yale! I used to know Tommy Bronson."

"You did!" cried Ching, interested. "He lived in the room next to mine. Boy, could he play football! Greatest star we ever had. A good guy."

"He . . . he was a friend of my brother's."

"Hmm. Say! Was your brother the tennis star at MIT?"

"Yes."

Ching laughed delightedly. "I knew it! That name has been bothering me ever since I heard it. Why, I played Bob Weston for the intercollegiate tennis championship one year!"

"You did? Why, then you must be Ching Tze-chang, the lightning Oriental!"

"That's me," said Ching. "I been swapping serves with these Japanese ever since. They got a return that smokes, too, let me tell you."

That recalled her from the green courts of ten thousand miles away and settled upon her again the heavy, dragging weariness of her hopeless situation.

"Where is he going?"

Ching grinned at her and his gold teeth sparkled. "Oh, no use holding it out on you. He's probably going up to Jehol to see if he can get the facts about Bob Weston. What was he doing up there?"

"Prospecting."

"An MIT engineer prospecting? Aw, you're kiddin' me!"

"No, that's the truth. He had strange ideas about what lay there. He would not even confide in me because he knew I would laugh at him—or he felt that I would. He made it very mysterious. And then this *Akuma-no-Hané*—"

"You're on the wrong track there," defended Ching. "The Devil With Wings had nothing to do with it. Not on your life!"

She did not believe him and it was plain from her glance that she knew he spoke out of loyalty and not knowledge. She had seen *Akuma-no-Hané* in action.

"What does *he* do in this country?"

Ching stopped smiling and became interested in his Matsubi's belts.

"Is it as mysterious as all that?" she persisted. "Japan would not offer these posters with the reward unless there was some truth in it. They say he bombed—"

"They credit him with everything that happens."

"Doesn't he do *any*thing?" she said scornfully.

"Sure he does. He *has* to!" snapped Ching in annoyance. "Sure. He's bombed railroads and shot down planes and killed men. But he didn't want to."

"Then why did he do it? Is he freelancing this career of terror?"

"No!" said Ching hotly.

"There was some talk in the streets of Port Arthur that your Devil With Wings was intent on dethroning the sovereign of Manchukuo, Pu Yi."

"How did you find that out?" exclaimed Ching.

She smiled and he knew he had dropped neatly into her trap.

"No fear," said Patricia. "I heard a rumor that somebody would like to. Is it some huge espionage ring?"

"Nuts," said Ching. *"Akuma-no-Hané* plays his hand alone."

"I heard," said Patricia sweetly, "that the Japanese and Russians had clashed on the banks of the Amur River."

"Somebody is always clashing on the Amur. Timur the Limper started his career there. Genghis Khan . . . Aw, what're you pumping me for?"

"No reason. But if Japan and Russia let this squabble grow into a war, then the world will dive in and it seems to me that Henry Pu Yi and the Japanese hold on the northern border of China would best be gotten out of the way in the event of such a catastrophe. Japan is endangering the peace of the Orient as long as Pu Yi stays on the throne."

"For a girl," said Ching with grudging admiration, "you got brains. You'd make a statesman, sure as hell."

"Thanks," said Patricia. "But I would feel easier if I knew where this killer was taking me."

"He isn't a killer!" cried Ching.

She smiled but small lights flared in the depths of her blue eyes. She had already formed her opinion of *Akuma-no-Hané* and it was not very nice.

Ching was sitting up straight, looking around the horizons for possible attack. It would come sooner or later. The communication of the Japanese was too swift and accurate to miss nailing them. Hidden dromes were scattered through this barren country like wasps' nests in the woods.

To confirm her disbelief, she said, "He wouldn't go through all this danger just because of me."

"He's done crazier things than that." Ching looked at her sharply. "What's all this monkey business about Confucius?"

She hesitated and then decided it would do no harm. "When . . . when Bob last wrote to me, he said that if anything happened to him I was to do everything I could to obtain a Confucius he was carrying."

"He *wrote* to you," said Ching.

"Yes. What's the matter with that?"

"Was there anything strange about the letter?"

"Why, no. Only that it was torn as though it had been censored."

"It *was* censored. The Japanese censor everything through this country. I don't even understand why they forwarded it to you at all. And you haven't any idea of what this Confucius means?"

"None. But it would be valuable if he would take such care to write me about it."

"Valuable enough to get him killed."

"Evidently your friend thought so."

"Aw, lay off *him*," squirmed Ching. "Haven't you got any brains at all?"

"You said just now I should have been a statesman."

"Sure, but you weren't talking about my boss. Besides, who ever heard of a statesman having any brains?"

Ching broke off and craned his neck nervously around the vast ring of the world, eyes probing into every cloud and trying to pierce each hill below.

"You don't look very much at ease."

He shook his head. "If the Japanese bumped your brother for that Confucius, they wouldn't give it up again without a hell of a fight."

"Are you afraid?"

"Me? Naw. But if they catch The Devil With Wings they'll . . . I guess we'd better not talk about that." He was silent for a while, searching the skies. "I don't like this. They act like they're saving their strength for a good hard wallop later on."

"Where?"

"Ask *Akuma-no-Hané*."

CHAPTER SIX

Shinohari's Trap

IMPERIAL Japanese Army Headquarters at Aigun vibrated to the grumblings of trucks which paraded endlessly up the crooked dusty street outside.

Some of the dust seeped in to lay grittily upon the desk and papers of Colonel Shimizu, commanding the Amur River Patrol.

The colonel, neat until it appeared that he must change his clothes every five minutes, sniffed daintily into his handkerchief and curled his thin lips into a feline grimace of distaste for noise and dust and activity. A mustard-colored greatcoat bulked through the door and the colonel glanced up with annoyance which quickly faded into welcome.

Intelligence Captain Ito Shinohari was too important in his field to have to stand on courtesy with mere line colonels. His greeting was curt—for a Japanese.

"I trust you have been well, Colonel," said Shinohari.

"Except for the noise and confusion, yes. And your own sacred health, Captain?"

"Excellent."

"May the Divine Beings favor you as they always have, Captain."

"May the Military Gods smile upon you, Colonel."

That finished, Shinohari pulled off his flying helmet and

began to strip the gloves from his thin, nervous hands. He lifted his pockmarked face and looked earnestly at Shimizu.

"Is there any news," said the captain, "of he who is called *Akuma-no-Hané*?"

The colonel's face lighted with surprised admiration. "Captain Shinohari, you amaze me! Yesterday I knew definitely that you were in Port Arthur. Today I have tidings of the white renegade and instantly you appear like a magician upon the scene."

"My business requires something more powerful than magic, Colonel."

"Indeed! Indeed so, Captain. If you wish to keep trace of your *Akuma-no-Hané.*"

"And the news . . . ?"

"A runner," said the colonel, "reports that *Akuma-no-Hané* landed last evening near the river, some fifty kilometers to the northwest. He was in company with the young Chinese with whom he associates and a young white woman. But tell me, Captain, why did I receive orders not to follow up such information? I could have taken a patrol . . ."

"Of course. I am sorry for the orders, Colonel. They were necessary. This time, it is imperative that he does not escape us. By the end of this week we'll have the pleasure of hanging his head by its ear in the main street of Port Arthur."

"Good! Good!"

"Before he has played his hand alone, Colonel. But this time he is encumbered with a young white woman, a Miss Patricia Weston."

"Robert Weston's sister?"

STORIES from the GOLDEN AGE

☐ Yes, I would like to receive my **FREE CATALOG** featuring all 80 volumes of the *Stories from the Golden Age Collection* and more!

Name _____

Shipping Address _____

City _____ State _____ ZIP _____

Telephone _____ E-mail _____

Check other genres you are interested in: ☐ SciFi/Fantasy ☐ Western ☐ Mystery

FREE SHIPPING!
NO PURCHASE REQUIRED

6 Books • 8 Stories
Illustrations • Glossaries

6 Audiobooks • 12 CDs
8 Stories • Full color 40-page booklet

- -

Fold on line and tape

IF YOU ENJOYED READING THIS BOOK, GET THE ACTION/ADVENTURE COLLECTION AND SAVE 25%

BOOK SET	**AUDIOBOOK SET**
~~$59.50~~ $45.00	~~$77.50~~ $58.00
ISBN: 978-1-61986-089-6	ISBN: 978-1-61986-090-2

☐ Check here if shipping address is same as billing.

Name _____

Billing Address _____

City _____ State _____ ZIP _____

Telephone _____ E-mail _____

Credit/Debit Card #: _____

Card ID # (last 3 or 4 digits): _____

Exp Date: _____/_____ Date (month/day/year): _____/_____/_____

Order Total *(CA and FL residents add sales tax)*: _____

To order online, go to: **www.GoldenAgeStories.com** or call toll-free **1-877-8GALAXY** or 1-323-466-7815

"Yes."

The colonel looked thoughtful and patted his stubby nose with the handkerchief. "Then you have spread the net of your entire intelligence force?"

"Yes."

"And you have a ring of steel around him even now, I presume?"

"If," said Shinohari, "your information about his landing is correct, he cannot escape by sky, land or water. The Gods of Destiny have ordained that his ruthless existence shall end in a matter of days, perhaps hours. You have my quarters ready for me?"

The colonel slapped his hands together and a short, smart orderly bounced like a jujitsu fighter into the room, to leap out of his final bounce into unbending attention.

"Take the Honorable Captain Shinohari to his quarters," said the colonel.

Shinohari followed the brisk orderly from the room. They emerged into the gathering softness of dusk and made their way down a street painted with the nervous light of guttering lanterns. The jostling soldiery made swift way for Shinohari and followed him with whispers and pointing fingers.

The orderly came to a clicking stop outside a low house which stood back from the busy street as though hiding itself in the purple gloom in fear of the military bustle of activity which stirred the town of Aigun on the Amur.

"If the Captain wishes me to remain . . ." began the orderly.

"I want nothing. Return to Colonel Shimizu."

The orderly saluted and Shinohari opened the door to step

inside. He fumbled for matches and then touched flame to the wick of a table lamp. The saffron flood spread out through the darkness, pushing back the shadows and finally driving them shivering into the farthest corners.

The light blinded the captain for a moment or two and he wrestled irritably with his greatcoat, getting it off. Finally he managed all the buckles and buttons and cast the weight of it from him to a low sofa.

Shinohari looked around then and froze into the paralysis of shocked surprise. His obsidian eyes bored across the light.

The Devil With Wings was seated indolently in a soft chair against the far wall. He was carelessly turning his .45 around and around in his black-gauntleted hands. An amused smile played in the corners of his mouth—the only visible portion of his goggle-masked face.

If Shinohari had been confronted with death personified, the agony of his amazement could not have been greater. He felt hot sweat start forth from his body and run, chilly, down his yellow flesh.

He felt all his energy draining from him as the sawdust comes running from a doll, to leave it flabby and shapeless. He began to rock slightly, trembling with the onset of hideously nauseating reaction.

Abruptly he collapsed into a chair behind him.

"Didn't you expect me, Honorable Captain?" said Forsythe. "I hardly thought you could do less. The fine boasts you have been making about hanging my head in the main street of Port Arthur were not, I hope, without point. You appear pale. Do not alarm me by saying you are in poor health."

"You . . . you are a *devil*!"

"Oh, come now. Can't I make a casual call . . . ?"

"How did you get here?"

Akuma-no-Hané smiled and the goggles flashed.

Shinohari's brain was beginning to function smoothly again. He glanced toward another red-covered couch and saw there the coat and uniform cap of a Manchukuo irregular officer. That took the superstition out of it.

"I am so sorry," said Shinohari, himself again, "that I had no slightest knowledge of your arrival. Oh, of course I knew you were in the vicinity, but to come here to the center of our strongest military post . . . You wished to honor me by requesting some small thing?"

Forsythe stood up, a terrifyingly tall figure to Shinohari. He still handled the .45 with lazy assurance. He did not pay Shinohari the compliment of keeping steady watch on the belted Luger at the officer's side. A bottle and two glasses stood under the lamp and Forsythe slowly began to pour out the drinks.

"The patrol may look in," said Shinohari. "Or headquarters may send a runner for me. Perhaps, for your own safety, you had best depart."

"Thank you for your consideration," replied Forsythe, knowing now that he ran little chance of being disturbed. He pushed a glass across the board to the Japanese. "Drink?"

"Certainly," smiled Shinohari, the color almost wholly back in his pitted face. He took the glass delicately and raised it in solemn salute. "May I drink to your success?"

"And may I drink to yours?"

Forsythe stood up, a terrifyingly tall figure to Shinohari.
He still handled the .45 with lazy assurance.

They drank.

"And now," said Forsythe, "you are probably curious about my visit, wondering why a man would risk running the lines even if his goal was to talk to such an important officer as yourself."

Shinohari acknowledged the compliment with a slight bow. "I admit there is some slight curiosity lingering in my mind. Won't you have another drink?"

Forsythe poured it out. "Again to your success, Honorable Captain." He put the empty glass back on the table. "You are having a bit of sport with the Russians, I see."

"Oh, not much more than usual. A few shots, a few men dead. Nothing of importance."

"No, of course not. What is a world war to an intelligence officer?"

Shinohari smiled. "You are very quick, Honorable Sir."

"If war does flare, Japan's position would be very admirable."

"Naturally," smiled Shinohari.

"Naturally," echoed Forsythe, grinning. "And your own financial position, Honorable Captain, would also be admirable."

"You allude to something definite?"

"I am not sure," replied Forsythe.

Shinohari wanted to divert this trend in the conversation but he showed nothing of it on his polite face. "May I ask if you have made your lovely traveling companion comfortable?"

"Quite. It was about her that I came to see you tonight, Captain Shinohari. You know of her brother, of course."

"Of course. A most regrettable situation, eh? And a most pitiable plight for the beautiful young lady. She has a powerful friend in you, *Akuma-no-Hané*!"

"Thank you. And while we are on the subject, would it be violating your military secrecy for you to tell me what you did with this brother?"

Shinohari's blank mask slipped for a fraction of a second. Blandly, then, he shrugged. "You flatter even me, Honorable Sir."

"Nevertheless," smiled Forsythe, spinning the .45 round and round until it was a glittering blue pinwheel in the yellow light, "nevertheless, I think it might be prudent for you to inform me of his whereabouts."

"There are many unmarked graves in Manchukuo, Honorable Sir."

"Ah, yes. And we have both had our share in filling them. But I do not speak of graves, Captain. I speak of a living man. Robert Weston. A young engineer of great promise . . ." Forsythe stopped, smiling placidly. "After all the favors we have exchanged, Captain, it would hardly be sporting for me to shoot you so ignominiously. Besides, once dead, you are not likely to talk. I regret the necessity of speaking about such crude things, but . . ." He shrugged and suddenly the .45 was motionless, muzzle centered on Shinohari's temple.

Shinohari studied the blankness of the goggles above the gun. There was something horribly unchanging about those lenses. They gave the impression that *Akuma-no-Hané* was capable of no feeling whatever. Shinohari's black gaze fastened upon the muzzle and he felt small hairs rise up along the back of his neck.

But the captain was calm. "I am afraid I must disclaim all knowledge of this young man, Honorable Sir. One in my position, even though lowly, cannot keep constant watch upon all persons in the land."

"Pardon," said Forsythe. "But you did not think for a moment that . . ." He drew the message from N-38 out of his pocket and tossed it down on the table. ". . . that I would believe this other than a misleading report destined for the files and the files only."

"My dear sir," said Shinohari complacently, "you are in error, I assure you. This you accuse me of is high treason."

"Yes," said Forsythe. "High treason against the Japanese government."

Shinohari was almost chuckling. "You rave insanely, *Akuma-no-Hané.* There is the message. It is from N-38 here at Aigun, and you found it on file in Port Arthur. No signature, nothing to make it valuable or believable to any power under the stars."

Forsythe was smiling broadly. Very softly, he said, "Only one thing has slipped your mind, Captain. Two months ago, here in the Amur section, your N-38 attempted to knife me as I slept. I shot and killed him."

"Yes," shrugged Shinohari. "But . . ."

Forsythe's voice became a monotone. "Yes, two months ago here on the banks of the Amur, N-38 died. And Robert Weston did not reach the Amur until two weeks after that event."

A cold, sharp knife of realization went twisting through Shinohari's questionable heart.

"The report here," said Forsythe, indicating the paper, "was never filed by N-38 but by the only man who had access to those files. Yourself, Captain."

Shinohari said nothing. He could think of nothing.

Forsythe was not smiling now. "You wanted that report to be false because you have your own personal reasons for Robert Weston's drop from sight.

"Where is Weston?"

Shinohari was tense. His midnight eyes were set and staring, out of focus, at the gun.

"And while you are answering that," said Forsythe, "you can give me the Confucius you took from him."

Shinohari still sat without speaking. His nervous hands had frozen about the arms of his chair and he held himself partly pushed forward. Abruptly he sagged back, clawing at his collar with a long yellow finger.

"I know nothing about that."

Forsythe paced around the table like a stalking panther. The black goggles were boring straight through into the captain's shivering brain.

Shinohari suddenly chanced a draw. The Luger rasped as he yanked it forth.

A clean blow to the yellow jaw, a splintering of wood and the crash of his body shook the room. Forsythe reached out and yanked the man to his feet.

Forsythe was not talking now. He had seen a bulge under the mustard-colored jacket. He ripped away the buttons and grasped the hard surface of a small doll.

He threw the captain backwards to the couch and went toward the light. He paused and looked closely at the image.

It was brown, pinpricked with wormholes. The shiny lacquer had worn away long ago, leaving the bare wood in patches like scars. Confucius had been carved holding his staff. A placid smile was on the bearded face. Forsythe gave the philosopher a cold grin of triumph in return. He thrust the image into his pocket and turned again to face Shinohari.

"High treason," said Forsythe. "The penalty, for you, would be very severe. I think you would find that it hurt to be a figure of scorn where you have been such a hero. Had I better shoot you now out of kindness?"

Shinohari's nerve was coming back. He was trying to gather enough courage to bluster his way out.

"You have no evidence!" cried Shinohari. "You are trying to intimidate me. You know nothing about . . ."

Forsythe's grin had the freezing capabilities of liquid air, showering down upon the luckless captain.

"Shinohari," said Forsythe, "we have matched wits too long to underestimate each other. You cannot help yourself by bolstering false hopes. From the moment I stepped into this Weston puzzle I knew your records were false. I have tried to find out why you hid truth from your own government. The only answer is that you did this for personal gain. Your pay is not high, your position makes large demands upon your salary. A less astute person would falsify his reports like a common burglar and rob the cash box with erroneous expense accounts. But not you.

"You have been playing your cards to make yourself wealthy. Oh, don't deny it. Robert Weston located a mineral deposit of great wealth. His find was immediately reported to you by your own agents. Instead of relaying this information to your government, you sidetracked it for your own interest, spiked all possible leaks. You did not kill Robert Weston because he was valuable to you personally.

"Greedy for the reward which you thought your work and position demanded, you have taken matters into your own hands. Somewhere near the Amur at this very instant, Weston is working for you under heavy guard—and your superiors know nothing about it. That, Captain, is treason. The reward for treason is death and disgrace.

"But have no fear about my reporting this to your war office."

At this the wilted Japanese showed swift signs of hope.

Forsythe knifed them instantly. "No, not to *your* war office, but to the military intelligence of another nation."

"You'll sell me out?" shrieked Shinohari.

"You have sold yourself out. Your price for being good is your life and your reputation. To cover this treason you pinned a crime on me—a crime which was never committed. Repaying that, I am holding your life in my palm."

Shinohari was thoroughly beaten down. He was a pile of mustard-colored cloth, sagging hopelessly.

Forsythe clothed himself in the irregular officer's greatcoat, turning up the collar and pulling down the cap until they almost met in effective disguise.

He went to the door and halted there for an instant to turn

and click his heels in a stiff and mocking bow. He stepped out into the thick gloom and was gone.

Shinohari sat shivering, yellow fingers pulling weakly at a loose thread on his jacket. Abruptly he was animated with mixed decision and terror. He sprang up and snatched the field phone from its hook.

"Colonel Shimizu!" cried Shinohari. "I have seen *Akuma-no-Hané*! Send out immediate orders to all troops and pilots to be on the alert! Give orders for them to shoot the renegade on sight and shoot to kill! HE MUST DIE BEFORE DAWN!"

CHAPTER SEVEN

The Secret of Confucius

MORNING had come to spread its yellow flood across the restive reaches of the Amur River. The three huts which huddled close beside the muddy bank of the twisting stream seemed to be without occupants or hope of ever having any, so squalid was their condition.

A staccato sound grew in volume to mingle with the lapping rush of the river. A cloud was churning skyward from the trackless plain and a plunging dot grew in size as it approached the huts.

Forsythe slewed the mustard-colored motorcycle to a stop beside the stream and looked cautiously at the three houses. No shots greeted him and, reassured, he drew off the irregular officer's now very dusty coat and cap and lashed them to the handlebars close beside a small pennant there which, in Japanese, indicated the machine to be the property of "Staff Dispatch. Japanese Imperial Army Headquarters. Aigun."

Forsythe kicked the stand up and twisted the grip. The engine raced wildly and he ran with it toward the yellow flood. At the bank he let go.

The motorcycle bellowed outward into the air, curved down and vanished with a dirty, spluttering splash. The river swept onward, leaving not a ripple to mark the spot.

Forsythe adjusted his goggles. What was visible of his face looked white and strained and weary. But as he walked toward the first hut he summoned up the energy to grin.

Before he reached the door it opened and Ching stepped out.

"The next time you beat it off like that," said Ching, "I'm going with you, girl or no girl. I couldn't sleep all night! How did you make out?"

"I talked with Shinohari," said Forsythe. "And he generously gave me . . ."

He hauled the Confucius from his jacket pocket.

"You got it!" cried Ching. "Quick! Lemme see!"

Forsythe gave it over, suddenly disinterested in it and very interested in Patricia, who was peering over Ching's shoulder. She showed the worry of a dangerous night but even this could not sap the vibrant vitality of her.

Forsythe thrust Ching aside and stepped into the room. He pulled off his gauntlets and cast them to the table. He turned, smiling, to Patricia.

"Your brother is alive."

Her eyes on him were wide and blank as she tried to understand what he had said. She did not move or speak.

"He's alive," said Forsythe, "and the key to his whereabouts is in that Confucius."

He said it very casually and then turned away from her to give her a chance to collect her startled thoughts.

A North Chinese with a face as impassive and yellow as brass was standing beside a small Primus stove, waiting to be recognized by Forsythe. He was one of many such subagents and his position was that of caretaker for these huts which appeared so abandoned but which were, in reality, an outpost and fueling station and hangar.

"Lin," said Forsythe, "do you think you could cook me up some ham and eggs? I'll need them before the day is out."

Lin almost smiled but not quite. He was flattered by the request and went swiftly to work with the Primus and a frying pan. Forsythe walked through a curtained doorway and Patricia, looking after him at the swaying cloth, heard water splashing as Forsythe washed up.

She turned slowly to Ching and saw him still fondling the doll. In a small, wondering voice, she whispered, "Bob's alive!" The dawning realization had taken minutes to drive away the chill certainty of her brother's death.

Abruptly, she shouted, "He's alive!" She grabbed the startled Ching and hugged him. She danced around the table and gave Lin a giddy spin across the floor. And then she left them both and stood outside the curtain looking at it with glowing, excited eyes. In every flowing curve of her graceful body she showed thankfulness and admiration.

But Forsythe did not come out and Patricia danced back to the table and began to set his place for him.

While she was doing this, a small cloud drifted over the brightness of her face. She laid the plates more slowly and then stopped with one held in midair, looking oddly back at the curtained door. No thought could be dark enough to hide her jubilance, but still she was troubled.

Had *Akuma-no-Hané* gone to this trouble for her alone?

No. Everything she had ever heard about him belied the fact that he had.

The Confucius was valuable.

Yes, very valuable.

Suddenly it came coldly over her that she and Bob Weston were less than pawns in a struggle much greater than their own small triumphs and fears. And *Akuma-no-Hané*, obviously, had only availed himself of an opportunity to strike at Shinohari.

She sat down slowly and watched Lin frying ham and eggs.

Forsythe came out. Perhaps if he had returned in his shirt sleeves without his helmet, her reaction would have been different. But he evidently could not chance her seeing his face and though he smiled, the oval lenses, glinting at her above the smile, sent lances of misgivings through her.

Forsythe slid into a chair across from her, regarding her curiously. "What's the matter? Didn't you hear me? Bob Weston is alive and you'll see him before night."

She managed a faint "Thank you," and then averted her glance to her plate.

Forsythe shrugged and turned to Lin who was ladling out the food.

Ching, in the meanwhile, had been rolling the Confucius around and around in his hands, studying it with lowered brows and pursed mouth. He began a systematic tapping and, when that failed to bring anything important to view, carried the image over to Lin's larder. Ching took some flour and rubbed it on the ancient wood. Suddenly a white line appeared around the base where the detachable portion had made the smallest imaginable crack.

Excitedly he unscrewed the base and produced a small, tight roll of paper. He started to open it when he glanced at Forsythe.

"I believe," said Forsythe, "that the letter is addressed to the young lady—if you don't mind, Ching."

She took it from Ching's reluctant fingers. Forsythe gave his whole attention to his eating, quite as though the matter was of very small importance.

Patricia read it once to herself and then glanced sideways at Forsythe. She knew he would take it from her in any case despite his original politeness in the matter.

She looked back and read it aloud.

Dear Sis:

I think we've got a bonanza! I've gotten out something like eighty thousand dollars in two weeks' work and there's chances to get more. I found an old dredge which came from god-knows-where and a crew of Japanese colonists are working it for me under my direction. In case anything happens to me and should this ever reach you, I have buried the eighty thousand in dust at the foot of a white rock which has a profile like an old man's face. We won't have to worry about *anything* anymore!

She turned to Forsythe again. "You . . . you really think he's alive?"

"Certainly," said Forsythe, pushing back his plate. "I've thought it all along."

"But how could you know unless . . ."

"He's an engineer, isn't he? You also know of that dredge, Ching."

"Sure I do," cried Ching. "An American brought it upriver chunk by chunk and assembled it. But his men revolted and he had to skin out with nothing much more than his life. Why, that thing's been there for ten years!"

"We'll find him at the dredge," said Forsythe. "Working." He stood up and made a gesture toward the door. "Roll out the ship, boys. We've got to fly about a hundred kilometers. We'll start in a few hours and meantime we can check over the crate. You're through at this stand, Lin."

Lin's brass face lifted worriedly. "You not come back? No wantchee this place no more?"

"No."

"You . . . you got a dream?" persisted Lin.

"A hunch?" Forsythe laughed, but there was a false note in his voice.

Ching was alarmed. "Hey, are you kidding me or what? You've gotten hunches about getting bumped off before."

"Not like this one," said Forsythe quietly, lighting a smoke. "Never mind. Let's start working on the ship."

CHAPTER EIGHT

The Wings of Death

THE silver attack plane's engine battered the surface of
the Amur, so low that the slipstream sent yellow waves
leaping back from the blast of passage.

The yellow day was nearing a hazy close and long streamers
of red had begun to creep toward the zenith like wounds in
the cobalt of the sky.

The ship was badly overweighted and no one knew as well
as Forsythe that an attack against it in number would result
disastrously for himself.

Ching had rigged a board across the roomy gunner's pit
and Lin sat there, eyes glazed, looking at the river lashing
out behind them like a saffron snake.

Patricia and Ching were crowded together on the gunner's
seat. The girl was so enrapt with the anticipation of seeing
her brother that she did not mind being crowded—in fact she
hardly noticed it.

Only Ching and Forsythe knew how they were raising
the odds against themselves. But without beacons by which
to land they could not go at night, and though they could
feel the intensity of spying eyes behind every rock along the
riverbank, and though they could sense the passage of radio
waves which told of their going, it was for Forsythe to order
and Ching to obey.

Suddenly a flash of light against the setting sun caused Ching to glance westward. He stiffened, eyes nailed to the far-off brace of dots which grew in size even as he watched.

He seized the inter-cockpit phone. "Kawasaki pursuits coming!"

Forsythe's goggles flashed redly as he glanced up. His black gauntlet yanked back on the stick and the attack shot skyward with diminishing engine pitch. It leveled out at two thousand. The Japanese ships were still boring in.

Forsythe gripped the phone. "Buckle your belts and leave your machine guns alone! I'll handle this from the front."

Ching nodded though Forsythe could not see. Ching could not have said a word at that moment. Forsythe knew he was going to die. That time seemed to be coming all too soon.

"Do you think they'll attack us?" said Patricia, trying to appear calm.

Ching nodded and tightened his belt. He had Lin hold on solidly to the drum racks.

The Japanese ships were spaced one above the other. With the sun streaming crimson around them, they climbed steadily to gain the best advantage of their foe.

Forsythe clamped the earphones over his helmet and twisted a dial to get the Japanese signal band.

A falsetto voice shrieked in upon him. A pilot was calling his headquarters.

"He is sighted! Shall we attack or wait?"

There was a pause and then, "ATTACK! Captain Shinohari is taking off immediately and should be there within two hours."

The phone clicked off but Forsythe let it crackle in case other orders whipped across the flaming sky.

The planes were high above them now, banking, starting to come over the top and down.

Patricia saw the blurring flash of the props stabbing straight at her. Above the roar of tortured steel she heard the shattering crescendo of machine guns.

The Kawasakis dropped like shot gulls out of a sky the color of flame, spattering long black lines which wove a spider's web about the attack plane. Tracer shredded as their props blasted through it.

Down, down, down, gun and engines going full and raving.

Forsythe held it until it seemed the Japanese would smash them out of the sky. And then, abruptly, Forsythe stabbed the nose of the attack skyward, straight at the nearest prop.

Louder guns battered at Patricia's ears and she knew they were Forsythe's. She looked straight ahead, conscious of the world upended crazily and twisting further yet.

In the blink of an eye the Japanese planes had vanished, but even before she realized it, the world had tipped over in the other direction like a mad compass being rocked wildly on its gimbals.

She had a sick sensation as the bottom dropped out. Centrifugal force crushed her into the pit, and then as they banked violently she felt herself flung against the retaining cleats of the Matsubi.

She had shut her eyes and now she opened them again to see the Rising Sun emblazoned on a fuselage straight ahead. The Japanese was rolling down and away, broadside to them.

They spanned the distance like a horse taking a hurdle and suddenly the Japanese was gone.

Patricia lightened and pressed upward against the belt; the bottom was falling out again. Her ears ached to the screaming blast of engines and guns. She was choked with acrid cordite and felt blinded with noise.

Straight over her head she saw a Japanese plane. It was upside down. Straight over her head—and yet the earth was there and the Amur was a flash of yellow in the sun.

An unseen fist slammed her down again and the earth was gone, the plane was gone. She was clutching the cowl so hard that pain was white-hot in her fingers. But she dared not let go.

Slammed bodily against cowl, Ching, seat and belt, head whirling as she strove to keep her long-gone sense of balance, she glimpsed the tail of a ship straight ahead. She heard Forsythe's guns open up.

She was crushed downward once more. She looked up as they looped. There was the plane, inverted, overhead, against the earth. As she stared, it fell off on one wing. Streamers of smoke, like a stab of ink through white water, shot from the reeling plane.

She saw a Japanese with a parachute pack trying to get out and then sky had replaced the sight.

Far off she heard the triphammer chatter of machine guns. The horizons tipped smoothly and whirled like a merry-go-round. The remaining Japanese plane was coming head-on, trying for a last resort—a collision.

Forsythe hurdled it. The earth tipped the other way and

then slid upward in a long sheet of brown and green and yellow until it was on top of them.

Machine guns were loud. Forsythe was firing once more. Patricia opened her eyes. The vision of a punctured Rising Sun fled across her sight, gone in an instant.

The world went right once more. The left wing slapped over to point at the earth and the attack flew smoothly around and around, seeming to stand still while the earth spun.

Forsythe stayed there for a full minute, turning, looking over the side with the dying sunlight crimson on his goggles.

Patricia followed his gaze. She could hear a screaming chant dimly through her engine-deafened ears. She had to look closely at the earth to see it.

Abruptly a whole hill exploded. Wings and tattered fabric blasted outward from a violent ball of smoke and flame. The concussion reached them like an easy bump.

Forsythe evened out the attack and started in a slow dive back toward the river. She could see his goggles flashing as he looked around the sky.

Suddenly she felt very sick. Weakly she steadied her head in her hands, sobbing.

Ching was beaming at the earth behind them. He turned with a grin and said, "No chance of him slipping, *yet*! He sure nailed those devils!" He saw her, then. "Hello, what's wrong? Yeah, I know. You can't tell which is up yet. Cheer up. We're almost there!"

CHAPTER NINE

Shinohari's Squadrons

WITH dusk hazy upon the earth under a scarlet-bannered sky, they sighted the dredge.

It stood in a backwash of the Amur and looked like some gigantic animal skeleton of prehistoric days propped up in the black water. The chain buckets were running up and returning empty in an endless stream. Water poured out from pipes and steam rose busily over the shacks on the deck of the barge.

Forsythe banked once around it, flying low. He could see men diving hastily down the swinging catwalk which connected the dredge with the shore. Another man in a white shirt stood on the deck, staring up.

Forsythe stabbed away from there like a silver arrow and picked up a nearby field. Gun cut and wires shrilling, he settled down for a landing upon the dark ground.

Before the ship stopped rolling, the man in the white shirt was seen sprinting over the river bank toward them. No one else could be seen anywhere. The top of the dredge was visible against the sunset of yellow and flame, and Forsythe, looking at it, thought of the gallows.

The man in the white shirt bobbed up beside the pilot's pit. He was young and tanned and eager, eyes bright with hope. Eyes as courageous and swift as Patricia's.

"Hey, what's it all about?" cried Bob Weston. "One glimpse of your crate and those cutthroats ran like quail yellin' *'Akuma-no-Hané*!'" He glanced away before Forsythe could answer and incredulity flooded in upon him to hold him for a frozen instant of amazement. Joy exploded in him and with a whoop he leaped up into the stirrup so hard that the ship rocked. He pried up the hood.

Patricia grabbed him and held him tightly as he lifted her down to earth. They said nothing because they couldn't talk. Patricia's eyes were shining with tears and happiness as she held him off and looked at him.

Forsythe, looking down at them, felt suddenly cold and lonely. She would never look at him that way. Never.

Ching and Lin got out and scouted with drawn automatics up to the bluff and lay there, protected by the edge, looking all around for possible ambush.

Bob Weston finally subsided enough to turn and shout at Forsythe: "Gee, you don't know how I want to thank you! Those guys went out of here as though they'd been shot from guns. Say, what was that they were shouting about?"

"It means 'The Devil With Wings,'" said Patricia slowly.

Bob's eyes grew big and he gaped with amazement, releasing his sister and taking a step back.

Ruffled slightly, Forsythe growled, "I don't bite."

"Oh, I didn't mean anything. But . . . but gee! I've heard about you so much since I've been up here I . . ." He was still backing away. He dragged his eyes from Forsythe's goggles and turned to stare his question at Patricia.

"He . . . he kidnaped me and brought me up here," she began.

Anger clouded Bob's imperious face but before it could spread to action, she caught his arm.

"Please," she begged. "You don't understand. I don't either. He's doing something against the Japanese and we . . . we sort of fit into the plan. I . . . I think he'll let us go free."

Darkness was dropping steadily upon them. The mist was curling whitely up from the river in the still air. Forsythe stood wearily up in his pit, looking at Patricia. She could never know the blow her tone had dealt him.

Even in the thickening gloom, the trickle which ran sluggishly down the front of his black jacket showed a glossy red like a streak painted there with lacquer.

He dropped to the ground, landing heavily and reaching out for the stirrup to support himself. He straightened up then. Fumbling inside his leather coat for a cigarette, he brought out the pack. It was soggy. He stared at it for an instant and then crumpled it in his hand. Drops of red dripped from the end of his fingers very slowly as he held them out, watching the blood fall.

Ching came back, gun in hand.

"They've beat it," said Ching. "Do you think those ships got word through to their headquarters?"

"I heard it," said Forsythe tonelessly. "Shinohari is on his way."

"He'll bring squadrons with him!" cried Ching. "We'd better take off quick!"

"No," said Forsythe. "I . . ."

"You're hit!" cried Ching. "Wait. Let me see!"

Forsythe thrust him back and left a dark print on Ching's white jumper.

Patricia and Bob, standing together, saw the streak which ran so slowly on the black leather of the jacket. Patricia clung hard to Bob's arm. Her face was a pale heart in the dropping night.

"You've got gold?" said Forsythe to Bob Weston.

"If you've come for that, I can't stop you from taking it," replied Bob dispiritedly. "I bought this dredge sight unseen with my last cent down in Port Arthur. And I no more than started it going when a little guy with a pockmarked face barged in and took over. He put Japanese soldiers to work with me and made me show them how. I . . . I thought for a minute there I was saved."

His voice grew sharper. "Yes, I've got gold!" cried Bob. "Three hundred and fifty thousand dollars in dust! Take it!"

Forsythe was standing erect with an effort. "Take it easy, lad. This ship wouldn't carry an extra hundred pounds, much less thousands. Is there a car across the river?"

"No, but there's one on this side and a bridge," replied Bob doubtfully.

"You've got gas for it?"

"Sure. *I* haven't used any."

Forsythe looked up at the darkening sky. A pale amber haze to the east showed where the moon would shortly appear.

"You haven't got too much time," said Forsythe. "Load your gold into the car and get across the river into Russia."

"But there's fighting around here," protested Bob.

"That fighting was ordered to cover up this gold operation." Forsythe smiled and fished absently again for a cigarette. He remembered then and brought his wet fingers back before him. "Not even the Imperial staff knows about this thing, Weston."

"But I thought the Japanese government . . ."

"Never mind that," said Forsythe wearily. He fumbled in his pockets and finally brought out a card. "Here. Take this. When you reach the railroad, show them this and bribe the officials. Get to Vladivostok. Ching will make sure you get through."

"What's that?" said Ching quickly.

"You're going with them. Both you and Lin," said Forsythe.

"But what about you?" demanded Ching.

Forsythe glanced up at the sky. "I have an appointment very shortly. With Captain Shinohari."

Patricia stifled a gasp.

Angrily Forsythe barked, "Get going! You've got until the moon rises."

"I won't leave you!" said Ching.

"You've got your orders."

Ching hung his head, trying to think of some way to change Forsythe's mind. But his mind was a whirl of despair. He finally reached into the rear cockpit and hauled out a small kit. From it he took a wad of bandages and handed them to the white man.

Forsythe tucked the gauze under his jacket.

Bob Weston was moving away, pulling Patricia with him.

"Wait," snapped Forsythe. "Come back!"

Bob and Patricia came closer to him and the glinting goggles stared blankly at them through the night.

"Weston," said Forsythe. "You'll wait for a little while—a few days—in Vladivostok. And if . . . and when I show up I can help you get your gold out of the country. Don't get me wrong. I want none of it. But . . . you didn't realize before that you were responsible for Miss Weston. You won't forget that again?"

Bob nodded wonderingly.

"And one more thing!" barked Forsythe.

Bob looked attentively as Forsythe sank down to sit on the catwalk. He wondered when he saw the black-garbed figure grinning at him.

"Give me your cigarettes," said Forsythe.

Hastily Bob brought a package forth and handed them over. Forsythe lit one and inhaled deeply. The red spark throbbed as he pulled on it again.

Suddenly Bob understood. He reached out his hand. Forsythe started to take it and changed his mind, shifting over to his left. And even then Bob felt the thick dampness which ran from the cuff to the back of the hand.

Bob turned and Patricia stumbled after him, looking back. Lin looked forlornly at Forsythe and then trudged away. Ching dallied, hoping Forsythe would forget his order.

"What are you waiting for?" roared Forsythe.

"Nothing," whimpered Ching.

"Get going. They need your help."

Ching turned very slowly and went around the wing. He stopped once, wanting badly to go back. But he did not dare.

When he reached the bluff above the river, Ching turned once more. He could see a glowing dot of red pulsating beside the vague outline of the ship.

Forsythe, sitting on the pack of his harnessed parachute, listened quietly. He had been hearing a far-off drumming sound for some time. It was distinct now, though still miles away.

He stood up and glanced southeast at the glowing sky, painted pearl with the rising moon. Shinohari was on his way with a score of ships at his back.

Forsythe ground the glowing coal of the cigarette into the dust and stepped wearily up to slide down into his pit. He kicked the engine into life and braked one heel to turn.

Full gun he streaked southeast, exhausts flaring against the night.

CHAPTER TEN

The Death of Akuma-no-Hané

THE car had crossed the river, heavy-laden, though the cargo in the black wooden boxes was very small. Bob Weston was driving across the open plain, setting his course by a star as engineers will.

Lin and Ching were kneeling on the back seat, looking upward and southward. They could see the pinpoint of red which was the attack ship's flaming exhaust and they could hear the drumming roar of many engines far away but coming nearer. Sadness and death were in their dark eyes as they watched.

Patricia turned to look at them and then followed their gaze. Her eyes were misty, sorrow lay heavily in her breast. "Ching. Did he . . . Is he doing that because the Japanese will think we are in the plane?"

"You didn't know that all the time?" said Ching bitterly.

"Then . . . then there isn't any chance of his getting away from them?"

"One plane against twenty?" said Ching angrily. "Not a chance! He knew he could never fly away from here alive. He *knew* it! *You* did that to him!"

Patricia looked startled.

"You know what I'm talking about," said Ching. "He's

85

doing this to let you get away. They'll never send a patrol to search for us after he's shot down. They'll think we all died with him. The men on the dredge are too far away to know what happened afterwards and they'll be too rattled to figure it out. One night of wind will hide the tracks this car is making. If he wasn't up there to hold them back, do you think, with all this border trouble, that the Japanese would stop on the river's other side? No. They'd find us and gun us by moonlight—and an easy job it would be. But they won't suspect, until it is too late."

Patricia suddenly hid her face in her hands, weeping. Ching's glare was merciless upon her shoulders.

"I didn't know," she whispered. "I . . . I thought I hated him. But it wasn't *hate*. It wasn't hate! And now I've let him go up there alone without ever telling him. . . ."

Ching was looking back. The moon was over the horizon now, bathing the world with an orange flood. Against it, like wasps, the Japanese pursuit ships were framed. And roaring down the sky to meet them went The Devil With Wings.

Forsythe, crouched in his pit, looked tiredly through his ringsights at the approaching armada. He clamped the phones on his ears and clicked his switch, getting the band of the Japanese.

He heard Shinohari's yelping voice crying, "There he is! That is he! Keep in close formation and dive past him in groups of three. Bow guns, then let the gunners get him. Don't pull up until you're far below. Turn then and climb above him again. Get him at all costs!"

Forsythe's lips curved downward into a twisted grin. He picked up the radiophone.

"Shinohari? *Akuma-no-Hané* speaking. If you'll let me land and discharge my passengers, I'll give up."

Shinohari's startled yip cracked through the phones. "Passengers? You say 'passengers'?"

"Bob Weston and his sister," replied Forsythe to the dot growing bigger in his ringsight.

He thought he heard a relieved chuckle. He had spoken in English because he was fairly sure no pilot in the squadrons ahead could understand it.

"You are too tricky," cried Shinohari in Japanese. "I cannot risk it. Military necessity demands your instant death."

In English, Forsythe said, "My death will not help you greatly, worthy Captain. Already word has been passed to certain powers and I think you will be wise enough to listen to their orders. I *know* you will. The evidence is too great and you cannot even resort to hari-kari."

Hurtling at each other across the palely glowing sky, enemy to enemy. And the man who was to die still held the winning hand.

Forsythe took off the phones. He did not want to hear more, he had nothing more to say. The crackle told him that Shinohari understood and that nothing could stop the hammering slugs which would soon riddle the attack plane.

He must be careful, Forsythe thought, not to fire. He did not know which ship was Shinohari's and Shinohari had to live. Living, to the captain, would be a fate far worse than flaming down into the dark earth far below.

87

Hands away from his trips, without even trying to get above his foes, Forsythe looked down toward the long silver strip which was the Amur River.

The exhaust stacks of the coming ships flared blue and red against the moon. The wings were spread out into groups, all compact, getting ready for their dives.

Forsythe looked up. Over his head a squadron started over the hump and stabbed down, engines screaming, scarlet pom-poms beating through their props.

Forsythe flew onward, keeping his course straight.

He was smiling.

The car was miles away by now and Bob was driving fast. Ching and Lin saw the exploding muzzles of the diving guns long before they heard the chattering roar.

By watching the direction of fire they made out the attack plane.

Ching's fists were balled tightly. His throat was dry and rasping as he whispered hoarsely, "Take some of them with you. Please take the captain. *Please . . .*"

Patricia was turned in the seat, staring up and back. She could not see distinctly. A shining film covered her eyes.

From afar they saw the attack plane burst into leaping yellow flames.

Like a comet it stabbed down the sky trailing fire, lighting up the wings of the greedy swarm about it.

Patricia tried to look away but she could not.

The brilliant arc of fire ended abruptly in the river and went out.

Like a comet it stabbed down the sky trailing fire,
lighting up the wings of the greedy swarm about it.

Ching was suddenly crazy but it lasted only a few seconds. He sagged back into the seat and stared at Patricia.

Belatedly they heard the long overdue whoosh and crash of the crumpled attack.

In a choked voice of disbelief, Lin whimpered, "He's dead."

CHAPTER ELEVEN

Vladivostok

IN a café just off the lobby of the Seven Flags Hotel in Vladivostok, Patricia, Bob and Ching sat at a table. A cosmopolitan crowd, made up with samples from half the races of the earth, jangled incessantly and moved restlessly up and down, ever changing, past the lobby door.

It was this which Patricia watched. There was no fire of hope in her eyes now. For five days she had delayed her brother with the faint hope that somehow, some way, *Akuma-no-Hané* had cheated death. The hope had dwindled to a spark which no longer fanned into a blaze when she fed her milling thoughts to it.

"You'd better eat something," said Bob concernedly. "Gee, you haven't been eating enough to keep a canary alive. And you haven't either, Ching."

Ching looked downheartedly at Bob and then shifted his weary gaze to Patricia. He saw she was watching the door and he too turned to look. But there was nothing there to hold her eyes except the changing crowd past the entranceway.

He looked back to her. At first he had hated her for what she had caused to happen, but now in his generous heart he could understand. He had tired of chanting to himself that he had been the one who had first brought her to Forsythe. He had wearied of telling himself that he should have sensed the omen held in that first meeting. It had been ordained by the gods from the very beginning that Patricia Weston would kill *Akuma-no-Hané*. No matter how it had been done. She . . . But he knew she was suffering. Everything was unreal to her, hazy, far away.

Bob turned to her. "There's a ship sailing this afternoon. I'm going to take passage on it and get you out of here." He started to rise but her hand reached up swiftly to catch his sleeve and pull him down again.

"No. He said . . . he said to wait."

Bob was impatient. "We've waited. We've stood on one foot and then the other for five days. I tell you I don't like to hang around. We've got a third of a million dollars left after all the bribes we've had to give and the sooner I get it aboard a ship under the Stars and Stripes, the better I'll feel about it."

But he sat down again and poured himself a drink. "Aw, I don't blame you, kid. That was a swell thing he—"

"Shut up," said Ching, tight-lipped, looking warningly from Patricia to Bob. Ching knew how close the girl was to cracking under the strain.

"Would . . . would he look for us here?" faltered Patricia, eyes never leaving the door.

Ching had answered it for her a thousand times. "Yes. He always comes to the Seven Flags Hotel."

"Always?" she said, snatching at hope again.

Ching looked down into his glass, conscious of her glance upon him, knowing she was begging him to give her something on which she could peg her confidence.

"There's no chance," said Bob. "We saw . . ."

Patricia suddenly tensed. Her eyes on the door grew wide.

Ching whipped around to look and to be hurled back in his chair by the force of his surprise.

A tall officer with pale yellow hair had stopped in the doorway to the café, to stand and rove his silver gray glance about the room.

His left arm was in a sling and the triangle of cloth almost hid the spreading gold wings of the flying corps and the half-dozen service ribbons on his tunic. Golden globes and anchors were on his collar and on the cap which he held in his right hand.

His face was smoothly shaven but none of the sprucing he had done could hide the tiredness in every line of him.

Suddenly he turned and saw the three at the table. Something happened to him. Life seemed to flow visibly back into him. A glow came to his face and glance as he straightened up and smiled.

He paced happily across the floor with eyes only for Patricia.

Until then she had not dared to be sure. She had never seen his face in full. But now, when she saw him smile and saw him walk, she *knew*.

She was crying then. Uncontrollable sobs were shaking her as she reached out and clung to him, pressing her face against his tunic.

His good right arm went around her and held her tightly.

For a long time no one said anything. They could not trust themselves to speak.

Finally Forsythe and Patricia sat down at the table, looking at each other. Ching pushed a drink into Forsythe's hand but Forsythe did not seem to know it was there.

Bob broke the silence. "Hey, how in the hell did you manage it?"

Forsythe did not hear him and Bob had to repeat his question.

"Parachute," said Forsythe absently, all his attention for the girl.

Ching diverted Bob's attention. "He had everything done in black. For the effect, see? Black parachute. Probably bailed out before they even started to fire. Locked his controls. Nothing to it for . . . Say, by the way," exclaimed Ching. "You don't even know his name, Patricia. Miss Weston, Captain Forsythe of the Royal Marines."

That also failed to shake them.

"But it's all over the Orient that you're dead," said Bob, still doubting the fact that Forsythe was alive.

Forsythe turned and smiled at him. "It's true and yet it isn't true. There's no further use for *Akuma-no-Hané*, Weston."

"Why not?"

Forsythe's smile broadened as he thought about it. "He's dead. And his work of keeping His Majesty informed of Japanese operations in the Far East is now being very efficiently done by a man who should know best of all."

"Who?" said Bob.

"By Captain Ito Shinohari of the Imperial Japanese Intelligence."

"But that can't be," said Bob. "I just read where they're

giving him a medal for killing you. The Order of the Rising Sun!"

Ching and Forsythe suddenly relaxed into a blast of laughter and then, by way of apology, Forsythe said to Patricia, "I passed along data about the man and unless he obeys and gives us intelligence service, he knows he will be forever disgraced. Yes, my work is being done. . . . But it isn't done at all. I've served my time in Intelligence and now I am back to the line. They tell me, Patricia, that I am being ordered to a nice quiet post in Bombay."

She looked at him with a smile which warmed him and sent small thrills of pleasure through him.

In a soft, caressing voice, she said, "I think I shall love Bombay."

Story Preview

Story Preview

NOW that you've just ventured through one of the captivating tales in the Stories from the Golden Age collection by L. Ron Hubbard, turn the page and enjoy a preview of *The Green God*. Join Lieutenant Bill Mahone, who is stationed in the besieged Chinese city of Tientsin—as Mahone starts to realize why the city is under attack, he begins a deadly quest to recover the Green God, a stolen sacred idol. Twists and turns lead inexorably to the grave of one General Tao, and a terrifying secret.

The Green God

SWIFTLY Lieutenant Bill Mahone of Naval Intelligence pulled his automatic from its shoulder holster and crawled along the side of the coffin, screening himself from possible guards.

Against the dark sky he could see the outline of the mound which marked the tomb of General Tao Lo, and around it the many unburied coffins which might or might not house the dead of Tientsin.

It was a dangerous mission that had brought Mahone venturing into the night. He had convinced his commander that they would not be able to stop the constant looting and murdering that had cast a reign of terror over the city until the Green God was back in its temple.

Tientsin's Native Quarter was half in flames; the dead were heaped in the gutters. The Chinese were convinced that their city would fall, now that their idol was gone. Before long these fanatics might sweep into the International Settlement and wipe it out.

Mahone had received a slip of paper that one of the natives in the Intelligence Department had brought in. It had been found in the Native Quarter, and the Chinese ideographs had read, "A jade calling card for General Tao Lo." The general

101

had been dead for a year, but Mahone was convinced that the Green God had been hidden in his tomb.

Now Mahone, disguised as a Chinese coolie, had come alone to try and get the Green God from the general's tomb and save the city before it was too late.

As he crawled along the side of the coffin a cry rang out directly above him and he felt the bite of a knife in his shoulder. With a spring he catapulted away and looked back. A dark figure leaped to follow him! Mahone's automatic spat fire and the shadow by the coffin screamed in agony. In front of him he could see other shadows rising up like ghosts. The faint light fell on the blades of many knives. Vicious snarls were hurled at Mahone as the guards swept down on him.

Knives flashed. The automatic spat again and again. There seemed no end to these fanatics. Bodies hurled their fighting lengths upon Mahone.

With his empty automatic he clubbed and beat about him. He could feel the impact of his steel crashing down upon skulls, arms, bodies. Chinese were sweeping over him in a stifling mass. Knives bit into his flesh like white-hot irons.

He felt men go down upon him, beside him, as he brought his gun butt down. But each time he struck, another screaming demon leaped to take the empty place. His arm was aching with exertion. He was bleeding from many wounds, but he fought on relentlessly.

Feet kicked him in the face, talonlike hands sought his throat, knives lanced in for his heart. His hand was sticky from the blood of crushed skulls.

By rolling over and over he managed to baffle the knives which flashed above him. Suddenly he brought up against a coffin. Then, protected on one side, he tried to gain his feet.

But each time he rose as high as his knees, a body would launch itself into him, pinning him again to the ground. He was partially protected by the inert Chinese he had either killed or knocked unconscious, and hope that he might be able to escape welled up within him.

His left hand fell upon the hilt of a knife and he snatched it up, lashing at the air before him. He felt that blade catch again and again, but each time, he pulled it from the flesh it had met and threshed out for new targets.

The knife blade was growing sticky and he felt a hot trickle of moisture running down inside his sleeve. The salty stench of blood was in his nostrils as he fought.

He was almost exhausted when the rush stopped momentarily.

To find out more about *The Green God* and how you can obtain your copy, go to www.goldenagestories.com.

Glossary

STORIES FROM THE GOLDEN AGE *reflect the words and expressions used in the 1930s and 1940s, adding unique flavor and authenticity to the tales. While a character's speech may often reflect regional origins, it also can convey attitudes common in the day. So that readers can better grasp such cultural and historical terms, uncommon words or expressions of the era, the following glossary has been provided.*

Aigun: a town in northern Manchuria, situated on the Amur River.

Amur River: the world's ninth longest river that forms the border between northeastern China (Manchuria) and the Russian Far East (between Siberia and the Pacific Ocean). It was an area of conflict during the war between China and Japan that began in 1937, and eventually led to World War II in the Pacific.

arc lamp: a lamp that produces light when electric current flows across the gap between two electrodes.

Bombay: a harbor and second largest city in India, located on the west coast of India and bordered by the Arabian Sea. Bombay was under British rule until 1947, when India gained its independence.

cordite: a family of smokeless propellants, developed and produced in the United Kingdom from the late nineteenth century to replace gunpowder as a military propellant for large weapons, such as tank guns, artillery and naval guns. Cordite is now obsolete and no longer produced.

cowl: the removable metal housing of an aircraft engine, often designed as part of the airplane's body, containing the cockpit, passenger seating and cargo but excluding the wings.

crate: an airplane.

drome: short for airdrome; a military air base.

Genghis Khan: (1162?–1227) Mongol conqueror who founded the largest land empire in history and whose armies, known for their use of terror, conquered many territories and slaughtered the populations of entire cities.

gibbet: an upright post with a crosspiece, forming a T-shaped structure from which criminals were formerly hanged for public viewing.

G-men: government men; agents of the Federal Bureau of Investigation.

Harbin: the capital and largest city of Heilongjiang Province, in northeastern China.

ideograph: a graphic symbol that represents an idea, rather than a group of letters arranged according to a spoken language, as in Chinese or Japanese characters.

inertia starter: a device for starting engines. During the energizing of the starter, all movable parts within it are set in motion. After the starter has been fully energized, it is engaged to the crankshaft of the engine and the flywheel energy is transferred to the engine.

International Settlement: a reserved area in China set aside by the government where foreigners were permitted to reside and trade. These areas, called settlements or concessions, were leased from the Chinese government and were administered by the foreign residents and their consuls and not under the jurisdiction of Chinese laws or taxes. All such foreign settlements on mainland China were eventually dismantled when the Communist Party of China took control of the government in 1949.

Jehol: a former province in northeast China; traditionally the gateway to Mongolia, Jehol was the name used in the 1920s and 1930s for the Chinese province north of the Great Wall, west of Manchuria and east of Mongolia. It was seized by the Japanese in early 1933, and was annexed to Manchukuo and not restored to China until the end of World War II.

jujitsu: an art of weaponless self-defense developed in Japan that uses throws, holds and blows. It derives added power from the attacker's own weight and strength.

Kawasaki: aircraft named after its manufacturer. Founded in 1918, Kawasaki built engines and biplanes in the 1930s, including fighters and bombers.

KDA-5: a fighter biplane built by Kawasaki, a Japanese aircraft manufacturer founded in 1918. The first prototype flew in 1932; 380 of these planes were built.

liquid air: air in its liquid state, intensely cold and bluish.

Luger: a German semiautomatic pistol introduced before World War I and named after German firearms expert George Luger (1849–1923).

Manchukuo: a former state of eastern Asia in Manchuria and eastern Inner Mongolia. In 1932 it was established as a puppet state (a country that is nominally independent, but in reality is under the control of another power) after the Japanese invaded Manchuria in 1931. It was returned to the Chinese government in 1945.

Manchurian: a native of a region of northeast China comprising the modern-day provinces of Heilongjiang, Jilin and Liaoning. Manchuria was the homeland of the Manchu people, who conquered China in the seventeenth century, and was hotly contested by the Russians and the Japanese in the late nineteenth and early twentieth centuries. Chinese Communists gained control of the area in 1948.

marten: a weasel-like forest mammal that is hunted for fur in some countries.

MIT: Massachusetts Institute of Technology; a private, coeducational research university located in Cambridge, Massachusetts. MIT was founded in 1861 in response to the increasing industrialization of the United States.

Mukden: the capital city of the China province of Liaoning in northeast China.

Nakajima: the name for the aircraft produced by the Nakajima Aircraft Company, Japan's first aircraft manufacturer, founded in 1917.

Native Quarter: Native City; walled portion of the city where the native Chinese resided, also referred to as the Walled City. Foreigners in Tientsin lived in the International Settlement, located outside the Native City.

Nippon: the native Japanese name for Japan.

Order of the Rising Sun: the second most prestigious Japanese decoration awarded for both civil and military merit.

pom-poms: antiaircraft guns or their fire. The term originally applied to the Maxim automatic gun (1899–1902) from the peculiar drumming sound it made when in action.

Port Arthur: a Chinese seaport surrounded by ocean on three sides. It was named after a British Royal Navy lieutenant who, during a war in 1860, towed his crippled ship into the harbor for repairs. The Russians and other Western powers then adopted the British name. Between 1904 and 1945 Port Arthur and the surrounding area were under Japanese rule.

Primus: a portable cooking stove that burns vaporized oil.

Pu Yi, Henry: (1906–1967) emperor of China (1908–1924) until he was expelled by revolution. In 1932, he was installed by the Japanese as the emperor of Manchukuo. At the end of World War II, he was imprisoned until 1959, when he was granted amnesty by the leader of the Communist government.

Rising Sun: Japan; the characters that make up Japan's name mean "the sun's origin," which is why Japan is sometimes identified as the "Land of the Rising Sun." It is also the military flag of Japan and was used as the ensign of the Imperial Japanese Navy and the war flag of the Imperial Japanese Army until the end of World War II.

Scheherazade: the female narrator of *The Arabian Nights*, who during one thousand and one adventurous nights saved her life by entertaining her husband, the king, with stories.

Shanghai: city of eastern China at the mouth of the Yangtze River, and the largest city in the country. Shanghai was opened to foreign trade by treaty in 1842 and quickly prospered. France, Great Britain and the United States all held large concessions (rights to use land granted by a government) in the city until the early twentieth century.

slipstream: the airstream pushed back by a revolving aircraft propeller.

snakeskin head, fiddle with a: an *erhu*; also known as the Chinese violin or Chinese two-string fiddle. It consists of a long vertical sticklike neck, at the top of which are two large tuning pegs, and at the bottom is a small resonator body (sound box) that is covered with python skin on the front end. The two strings are attached from the pegs to the base, and it is played with a horsehair bow. The *erhu* can be traced back to instruments introduced into China more than a thousand years ago.

Son of Heaven: Emperor of China; sovereign of Imperial China reigning since the founding of the Qin Dynasty in 221 BC until the fall of the Qing Dynasty in 1912. The emperor was recognized as the ruler of "All under heaven." Henry Pu Yi was the last reigning emperor of the Qing Dynasty.

Tientsin: seaport located southeast of Peking; China's third largest city and major transportation and trading center. Tientsin was a "Treaty Port," a generic term used to denote

Chinese cities open to foreign residence and trade, usually the result of a treaty.

Timur the Limper: (1336–1405) a name for Timur Lenk or Tamerlane meaning "Timur the Lame." Timur was a Mongol conqueror and the name is supposed to have reflected the battle wounds he received.

Toledo: Toledo, Spain; a city renowned for making swords of finely tempered steel.

tracer: a bullet or shell whose course is made visible by a trail of flames or smoke, used to assist in aiming.

Vladivostok: city and major port in southeastern Russia, on Golden Horn Bay, an inlet of the Sea of Japan. It is the last city on the eastern end of the Trans-Siberian Railway.

will-o'-the-wisp: somebody or something that is misleading or elusive.

L. Ron Hubbard
in the Golden Age
of Pulp Fiction

*In writing an adventure story
a writer has to know that he is adventuring
for a lot of people who cannot.
The writer has to take them here and there
about the globe and show them
excitement and love and realism.
As long as that writer is living the part of an
adventurer when he is hammering
the keys, he is succeeding with his story.*

*Adventuring is a state of mind.
If you adventure through life, you have a
good chance to be a success on paper.*

*Adventure doesn't mean globe-trotting,
exactly, and it doesn't mean great deeds.
Adventuring is like art.
You have to live it to make it real.*

—*L. RON HUBBARD*

L. Ron Hubbard
and American
Pulp Fiction

B ORN March 13, 1911, L. Ron Hubbard lived a life at least as expansive as the stories with which he enthralled a hundred million readers through a fifty-year career.

Originally hailing from Tilden, Nebraska, he spent his formative years in a classically rugged Montana, replete with the cowpunchers, lawmen and desperadoes who would later people his Wild West adventures. And lest anyone imagine those adventures were drawn from vicarious experience, he was not only breaking broncs at a tender age, he was also among the few whites ever admitted into Blackfoot society as a bona fide blood brother. While if only to round out an otherwise rough and tumble youth, his mother was that rarity of her time—a thoroughly educated woman—who introduced her son to the classics of Occidental literature even before his seventh birthday.

But as any dedicated L. Ron Hubbard reader will attest, his world extended far beyond Montana. In point of fact, and as the son of a United States naval officer, by the age of eighteen he had traveled over a quarter of a million miles. Included therein were three Pacific crossings to a then still mysterious Asia, where he ran with the likes of Her British Majesty's agent-in-place

L. Ron Hubbard, left, at Congressional Airport, Washington, DC, 1931, with members of George Washington University flying club.

for North China, and the last in the line of Royal Magicians from the court of Kublai Khan. For the record, L. Ron Hubbard was also among the first Westerners to gain admittance to forbidden Tibetan monasteries below Manchuria, and his photographs of China's Great Wall long graced American geography texts.

Upon his return to the United States and a hasty completion of his interrupted high school education, the young Ron Hubbard entered George Washington University. There, as fans of his aerial adventures may have heard, he earned his wings as a pioneering barnstormer at the dawn of American aviation. He also earned a place in free-flight record books for the longest sustained flight above Chicago. Moreover, as a roving reporter for *Sportsman Pilot* (featuring his first professionally penned articles), he further helped inspire a generation of pilots who would take America to world airpower.

Immediately beyond his sophomore year, Ron embarked on the first of his famed ethnological expeditions, initially to then untrammeled Caribbean shores (descriptions of which would later fill a whole series of West Indies mystery-thrillers). That the Puerto Rican interior would also figure into the future of Ron Hubbard stories was likewise no accident. For in addition to cultural studies of the island, a 1932–33

LRH expedition is rightly remembered as conducting the first complete mineralogical survey of a Puerto Rico under United States jurisdiction.

There was many another adventure along this vein: As a lifetime member of the famed Explorers Club, L. Ron Hubbard charted North Pacific waters with the first shipboard radio direction finder, and so pioneered a long-range navigation system universally employed until the late twentieth century. While not to put too fine an edge on it, he also held a rare Master Mariner's license to pilot any vessel, of any tonnage in any ocean.

Yet lest we stray too far afield, there is an LRH note at this juncture in his saga, and it reads in part:

"I started out writing for the pulps, writing the best I knew, writing for every mag on the stands, slanting as well as I could."

To which one might add: His earliest submissions date from the summer of 1934, and included tales drawn from true-to-life Asian adventures, with characters roughly modeled on British/American intelligence operatives he had known in Shanghai. His early Westerns were similarly peppered with details drawn from personal

Capt. L. Ron Hubbard in Ketchikan, Alaska, 1940, on his Alaskan Radio Experimental Expedition, the first of three voyages conducted under the Explorers Club flag.

experience. Although therein lay a first hard lesson from the often cruel world of the pulps. His first Westerns were soundly rejected as lacking the authenticity of a Max Brand yarn (a particularly frustrating comment given L. Ron Hubbard's Westerns came straight from his Montana homeland, while Max Brand was a mediocre New York poet named Frederick Schiller Faust, who turned out implausible six-shooter tales from the terrace of an Italian villa).

Nevertheless, and needless to say, L. Ron Hubbard persevered and soon earned a reputation as among the most publishable names in pulp fiction, with a ninety percent placement rate of first-draft manuscripts. He was also among the most prolific, averaging between seventy and a hundred thousand words a month. Hence the rumors that L. Ron Hubbard had redesigned a typewriter for faster keyboard action and pounded out manuscripts on a continuous roll of butcher paper to save the precious seconds it took to insert a single sheet of paper into manual typewriters of the day.

That all L. Ron Hubbard stories did not run beneath said byline is yet another aspect of pulp fiction lore. That is, as publishers periodically rejected manuscripts from top-drawer authors if only to avoid paying top dollar, L. Ron Hubbard and company just as frequently replied with submissions under various pseudonyms. In Ron's case, the list

---

A MAN OF MANY NAMES

Between 1934 and 1950, L. Ron Hubbard authored more than fifteen million words of fiction in more than two hundred classic publications. To supply his fans and editors with stories across an array of genres and pulp titles, he adopted fifteen pseudonyms in addition to his already renowned L. Ron Hubbard byline.

Winchester Remington Colt
Lt. Jonathan Daly
Capt. Charles Gordon
Capt. L. Ron Hubbard
Bernard Hubbel
Michael Keith
Rene Lafayette
Legionnaire 148
Legionnaire 14830
Ken Martin
Scott Morgan
Lt. Scott Morgan
Kurt von Rachen
Barry Randolph
Capt. Humbert Reynolds

included: Rene Lafayette, Captain Charles Gordon, Lt. Scott Morgan and the notorious Kurt von Rachen—supposedly on the lam for a murder rap, while hammering out two-fisted prose in Argentina. The point: While L. Ron Hubbard as Ken Martin spun stories of Southeast Asian intrigue, LRH as Barry Randolph authored tales of

L. Ron Hubbard, circa 1930, at the outset of a literary career that would finally span half a century.

romance on the Western range—which, stretching between a dozen genres is how he came to stand among the two hundred elite authors providing close to a million tales through the glory days of American Pulp Fiction.

In evidence of exactly that, by 1936 L. Ron Hubbard was literally leading pulp fiction's elite as president of New York's American Fiction Guild. Members included a veritable pulp hall of fame: Lester "Doc Savage" Dent, Walter "The Shadow" Gibson, and the legendary Dashiell Hammett—to cite but a few.

Also in evidence of just where L. Ron Hubbard stood within his first two years on the American pulp circuit: By the spring of 1937, he was ensconced in Hollywood, adopting a Caribbean thriller for Columbia Pictures, remembered today as *The Secret of Treasure Island.* Comprising fifteen thirty-minute episodes, the L. Ron Hubbard screenplay led to the most profitable matinée serial in Hollywood history. In accord with Hollywood culture, he was thereafter continually called

The 1937 Secret of Treasure Island, *a fifteen-episode serial adapted for the screen by L. Ron Hubbard from his novel,* Murder at Pirate Castle.

upon to rewrite/doctor scripts—most famously for long-time friend and fellow adventurer Clark Gable.

In the interim—and herein lies another distinctive chapter of the L. Ron Hubbard story—he continually worked to open Pulp Kingdom gates to up-and-coming authors. Or, for that matter, anyone who wished to write. It was a fairly unconventional stance, as markets were already thin and competition razor sharp. But the fact remains, it was an L. Ron Hubbard hallmark that he vehemently lobbied on behalf of young authors—regularly supplying instructional articles to trade journals, guest-lecturing to short story classes at George Washington University and Harvard, and even founding his own creative writing competition. It was established in 1940, dubbed the Golden Pen, and guaranteed winners both New York representation and publication in *Argosy*.

But it was John W. Campbell Jr.'s *Astounding Science Fiction* that finally proved the most memorable LRH vehicle. While every fan of L. Ron Hubbard's galactic epics undoubtedly knows the story, it nonetheless bears repeating: By late 1938, the pulp publishing magnate of Street & Smith was determined to revamp *Astounding Science Fiction* for broader readership. In particular, senior editorial director F. Orlin Tremaine called for stories with a stronger *human element*. When acting editor John W. Campbell balked, preferring his spaceship-driven tales,

Tremaine enlisted Hubbard. Hubbard, in turn, replied with the genre's first truly *character-driven* works, wherein heroes are pitted not against bug-eyed monsters but the mystery and majesty of deep space itself—and thus was launched the Golden Age of Science Fiction.

The names alone are enough to quicken the pulse of any science fiction aficionado, including LRH friend and protégé, Robert Heinlein, Isaac Asimov, A. E. van Vogt and Ray Bradbury. Moreover, when coupled with LRH stories of fantasy, we further come to what's rightly been described as the foundation of every modern tale of horror: L. Ron Hubbard's immortal *Fear*. It was rightly proclaimed by Stephen King as one of the very few works to genuinely warrant that overworked term "classic"—as in: *"This is a classic tale of creeping, surreal menace and horror. . . . This is one of the really, really good ones."*

To accommodate the greater body of L. Ron Hubbard fantasies, Street & Smith inaugurated *Unknown*—a classic pulp if there ever was one, and wherein readers were soon thrilling to the likes of *Typewriter in the Sky* and *Slaves of Sleep* of which Frederik Pohl would declare: *"There are bits*

L. Ron Hubbard, 1948, among fellow science fiction luminaries at the World Science Fiction Convention in Toronto.

and pieces from Ron's work that became part of the language in ways that very few other writers managed."

And, indeed, at J. W. Campbell Jr.'s insistence, Ron was regularly drawing on themes from the Arabian Nights and

121

so introducing readers to a world of genies, jinn, Aladdin and Sinbad—all of which, of course, continue to float through cultural mythology to this day.

At least as influential in terms of post-apocalypse stories was L. Ron Hubbard's 1940 *Final Blackout*. Generally acclaimed as the finest anti-war novel of the decade and among the ten best works of the genre ever authored—here, too, was a tale that would live on in ways few other writers

imagined. Hence, the later Robert Heinlein verdict: "Final Blackout *is as perfect a piece of science fiction as has ever been written.*"

Like many another who both lived and wrote American pulp adventure, the war proved a tragic end to Ron's sojourn in the pulps. He served with distinction in four theaters and was highly decorated for commanding corvettes in the North Pacific. He was also grievously wounded in combat, lost many a close friend and colleague and thus resolved to say farewell to pulp fiction and devote himself to what it had supported these many years—namely, his serious research.

Portland, Oregon, 1943; L. Ron Hubbard captain of the US Navy subchaser PC 815.

But in no way was the LRH literary saga at an end, for as he wrote some thirty years later, in 1980:

"Recently there came a period when I had little to do. This was novel in a life so crammed with busy years, and I decided to amuse myself by writing a novel that was pure science fiction."

That work was *Battlefield Earth: A Saga of the Year 3000*. It was an immediate *New York Times* bestseller and, in fact, the first international science fiction blockbuster in decades. It was not, however, L. Ron Hubbard's magnum opus, as that distinction is generally reserved for his next and final work: The 1.2 million word *Mission Earth*.

> **Final Blackout**
> *is as perfect a piece of science fiction as has ever been written.*
>
> —Robert Heinlein

How he managed those 1.2 million words in just over twelve months is yet another piece of the L. Ron Hubbard legend. But the fact remains, he did indeed author a ten-volume *dekalogy* that lives in publishing history for the fact that each and every volume of the series was also a *New York Times* bestseller.

Moreover, as subsequent generations discovered L. Ron Hubbard through republished works and novelizations of his screenplays, the mere fact of his name on a cover signaled an international bestseller. . . . Until, to date, sales of his works exceed hundreds of millions, and he otherwise remains among the most enduring and widely read authors in literary history. Although as a final word on the tales of L. Ron Hubbard, perhaps it's enough to simply reiterate what editors told readers in the glory days of American Pulp Fiction:

He writes the way he does, brothers, because he's been there, seen it and done it!

THE STORIES FROM THE GOLDEN AGE

Your ticket to adventure starts here with the Stories from
the Golden Age collection by master storyteller L. Ron Hubbard.
These gripping tales are set in a kaleidoscope of exotic locales and brim
with fascinating characters, including some of the
most vile villains, dangerous dames and brazen heroes
you'll ever get to meet.

The entire collection of over one hundred and fifty stories is being
released in a series of eighty books and audiobooks.
For an up-to-date listing of available titles,
go to www.goldenagestories.com.

AIR ADVENTURE

Arctic Wings	*Man-Killers of the Air*
The Battling Pilot	*On Blazing Wings*
Boomerang Bomber	*Red Death Over China*
The Crate Killer	*Sabotage in the Sky*
The Dive Bomber	*Sky Birds Dare!*
Forbidden Gold	*The Sky-Crasher*
Hurtling Wings	*Trouble on His Wings*
The Lieutenant Takes the Sky	*Wings Over Ethiopia*

FAR-FLUNG ADVENTURE

SEA ADVENTURE

TALES FROM THE ORIENT

MYSTERY

127

FANTASY

Borrowed Glory	*If I Were You*
The Crossroads	*The Last Drop*
Danger in the Dark	*The Room*
The Devil's Rescue	*The Tramp*
He Didn't Like Cats	

SCIENCE FICTION

The Automagic Horse	*A Matter of Matter*
Battle of Wizards	*The Obsolete Weapon*
Battling Bolto	*One Was Stubborn*
The Beast	*The Planet Makers*
Beyond All Weapons	*The Professor Was a Thief*
A Can of Vacuum	*The Slaver*
The Conroy Diary	*Space Can*
The Dangerous Dimension	*Strain*
Final Enemy	*Tough Old Man*
The Great Secret	*240,000 Miles Straight Up*
Greed	*When Shadows Fall*
The Invaders	

WESTERN

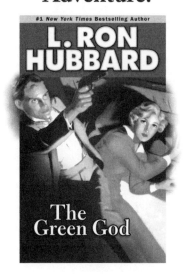

JOIN THE PULP REVIVAL
America in the 1930s and 40s

Pulp fiction was in its heyday and 30 million readers were regularly riveted by the larger-than-life tales of master storyteller L. Ron Hubbard. For this was pulp fiction's golden age, when the writing was raw and every page packed a walloping punch.

That magic can now be yours. An evocative world of nefarious villains, exotic intrigues, courageous heroes and heroines—a world that today's cinema has barely tapped for tales of adventure and swashbucklers.

Enroll today in the Stories from the Golden Age Club and begin receiving your monthly feature edition selected from more than 150 stories in the collection.

You may choose to enjoy them as either a paperback or audiobook for the special membership price of $9.95 each month along with FREE shipping and handling.

CALL TOLL-FREE: **1-877-8GALAXY**
(1-877-842-5299) OR GO ONLINE TO
www.goldenagestories.com
AND BECOME PART OF THE PULP REVIVAL!